Cats!

BZZZZ

Cats!

PURRFECT STRANGERS

SCRIPT **FRÉDÉRIC BRRÉMAUD**

ART **PAOLA ANTISTA**

COLORS **CECILIA GIUMENTO**

ENGLISH TRANSLATION **ANNIE GULLION**

LETTERING **MICHAEL HEISLER**

COVER ART **PAOLA ANTISTA** WITH **CECILIA GIUMENTO**

DARK HORSE BOOKS

PRESIDENT AND PUBLISHER **MIKE RICHARDSON**

COLLECTION EDITOR **FREDDYE MILLER** COLLECTION ASSOCIATE EDITOR **JUDY KHUU**

COLLECTION ASSISTANT EDITOR **ROSE WEITZ** DESIGNER **SARAH TERRY**

DIGITAL ART TECHNICIAN **ANN GRAY**

CATS! PURRFECT STRANGERS

Published by Dark Horse Books
A division of Dark Horse Comics LLC
10956 SE Main Street | Milwaukie, OR 97222

DarkHorse.com

To find a comics shop in your area, visit comicshoplocator.com

Library of Congress Cataloging-in-Publication Data

Names: Brrémaud, Frédéric, writer. | Antista, Paola, 1976- artist. | Giumento, Cecilia, colourist.
Title: Cats! : purrfect strangers / writer, Frédéric Brrémaud ; artist, Paola Antista ; colors, Cecilia Giumento.
Other titles: Chats!. English
Description: Milwaukie, OR : Dark Horse Books, 2021.
Identifiers: LCCN 2021000829 | ISBN 9781506726137 (trade paperback) | ISBN 9781506726151 (ebook)
Subjects: LCSH: Graphic novels. | CYAC: Graphic novels. | Short stories. | Cats--Fiction.
Classification: LCC PZ7.7.B787 Cat 2021 | DDC 741.5/944--dc23
LC record available at https://lccn.loc.gov/2021000829

First English-language edition: October 2021
Ebook ISBN 978-1-50672-615-1
Trade paperback ISBN 978-1-50672-613-7

10 9 8 7 6 5 4 3 2 1
Printed in China

ILLUSTRATION BY PAOLA ANTISTA WITH COLORS BY CECILIA GIUMENTO

HEE HEE HEE!
MEOOOW!
=HMPH= WE'LL SEE WHO HAS THE LAST LAUGH!

FLIT FLIT

MRROWW!
=HSSS HSSS=

ISN'T HE CUTE?
NO, HE'S HIDEOUS!

=HSSS HSSS=

YOU'RE JUST SAYING THAT BECAUSE YOU'RE JEALOUS!
I'M SAYING THAT BECAUSE I'VE BEEN BETRAYED BY MY BEST FRIEND!

TRAITOR!
TRAITOR!
TRAITOR!

TRAITOR!
TRAITOR...
AAATCHOOO!!!
GESUNDHEIT! HA HA HA!
=HSSS HSSS=
I GUESS ALL THIS DESERVES AN EXPLANATION, RIGHT?

MY NAME IS...
MANON! ARE YOU COMING TO EAT?!

I'M NOT EIGHTEEN YET, BUT I'M GETTING CLOSER BY THE DAY. I LIVE IN A SMALL TOWN NEAR THE COUNTRY...

NO, MOM, I HAVE TO PICK UP ERIKA AND THEN GO GET A PUPPY!

UNLIKE MY FRIENDS--WHO LIVE WITH THEIR PARENTS--I AM INDEPENDENT. WELL... ALMOST INDEPENDENT! THE TRUTH IS THEY LET ME MOVE INTO AN EMPTY ROOM THAT'S SEPARATE FROM MY FAMILY'S APARTMENT...

IT'S A NICE LITTLE STUDIO, NOT BAD AT ALL.

ERIKA'S MAGAZINES! IF I FORGET THESE, SHE'S GONNA HAVE A FIT...

ALL SET!

BYE, BUBBLES!

!

MOM, MANON'S GOING SOME-WHERE!

DON'T GET BACK TOO LATE, MANON...!
GRRR...

UGH, I'M FED UP! I'D LOVE TO BE KIKI FROM KIKI'S DELIVERY SERVICE AND NOT SEE MY FAMILY FOR A YEAR...

IN THIS NEIGHBORHOOD, I KNOW EVERYBODY.

MS. LUCIENNE, WHO FEEDS ALL THE STRAY CATS...

HELLO, MANON!
HELLO, MS. LUCIENNE!

THE JOLLY BROTHERS...
MEOOW

THEY HAVE A BAD REPUTATION, BUT I LIKE THEM...I EVEN HAVE A SOFT SPOT FOR THE YOUNGEST ONE.
HIYA, FRANKY!

HEY, MANON!

GET YOUR DIRTY PAWS OFF THAT, YOU THIEF!

PAF
OUCH!

YIPES! OWEEE! HAVE MERCY!
YOU'LL REGRET THIS, MISCREANT! I'M CALLING THE POLICE!
MEOOW
MEOOW

OOPS!

RIGHT ON TIME...

DING DONG!

IS THAT YOU, MANON...? JUST A SEC, I'LL BE RIGHT DOWN!

WELL?
WELL WHAT?

WHAT ARE YOU GONNA CALL YOUR DOG?

I'M WAITING UNTIL I SEE IT! MY PARENTS DID THE SAME THING WITH ME...

THEY WERE TRYING TO DECIDE BETWEEN MARICA, FRUFRU, AND MANON! WHEN THEY SAW ME, THEY KNEW RIGHT AWAY THAT MANON SUITED ME BEST!
WOW, THAT'S WILD...

WE'RE HERE!
AUNTIE HELEN, IT'S ME, ERIKA!!!

HI, AUNTIE!

THIS IS MY FRIEND MANON! SHE'S THE ONE WHO'S COMING TO PICK OUT A PUPPY!
YOU'LL SEE, THEY'RE WONDERFUL. MIRZA IS IN THE BARN.

YOU CAN GET CLOSER, SHE'S NOT MEAN!

?

MEW!

MEOOOWWWW!

HELLO, YOU...
WHY ARE YOU SAYING HELLO TO **HIM?** DON'T YOU SEE IT'S A STUPID CAT?

HE'S SO CUTE... THAT'S IT, MA'AM, I'VE MADE MY CHOICE!
WHAT?!

IT TOOK ME SIX MONTHS TO TALK HER INTO GETTING A DOG! IT WAS NOT SO WE'D LEAVE HERE WITH A CAT!

WELL, WHAT'S THE DIFFERENCE?
THE DIFFERENCE IS THAT THE KIBBLE YOU GIVE HIM ISN'T THE SAME...! THAT ALL THE BOOKS WE READ WERE A WASTE OF TIME!

AND MOST OF ALL, THE DIFFERENCE IS THAT...

AAATCHOOO!!!

HSS
HSS
...THAT I'M ALLERGIC TO CATS!

OKAY, SO WHAT ARE YOU GOING TO CALL HIM?
JUSTIN TIMBERLAKE?
PUDGY?
PUSS-PUSS?

I WAS THINKING GRAPEFRUIT, BECAUSE OF HIS COLOR!

GRAPEFRUIT...? WELL, I GUESS IT'S NO WORSE THAN PINEAPPLE...!

I'M SO HAPPY THAT ERIKA'S FINALLY ADOPTING A CAT.
YEAH, IT WASN'T EASY TO CONVINCE HER.
MMMM...

AT THE SAME TIME, I UNDERSTAND. SHE'S ALLERGIC TO CATS, AND ON TOP OF THAT, SHE'S ALWAYS DREAMED OF HAVING A DOG!
YUM... NOT BAD AT ALL...

ATCHOOO!

SHE'S HERE!
YOU KITTIES GET READY TO WELCOME A NEW FRIEND!

HEY, IT'S ME!
DID YOU BRING IT?
WHAT DO YOU THINK MADE ME SNEEZE LIKE THAT?

OH! HE'S SO CUTE!
REALLY? YOU THINK SO?

YOU'LL GET USED TO HIM, YOU'LL SEE...
DON'T WORRY, GIRLS, I'VE GIVEN UP ON DOGS! I PROMISE!

WHAT ARE YOU GOING TO CALL HIM?

UH...
FIDO! BOO-HOO-HOO...

MROWWW!
IT TOOK ME TWO WEEKS TO GET AN APPOINTMENT AT THE VET. HE'LL BE FURIOUS IF I'M LATE!
YES, I KNOW YOU'RE NOT IN A HURRY TO GET YOUR SHOT!
HEY, MANON!
ERIKA, WHAT A NICE SURPRISE! HOW'S IT GOING?
GREAT!
YOU KNOW WHAT? I FINALLY LIKE MY CAT!
EVEN NICER...!
I EVEN CHANGED HIS NAME. FROM NOW ON, HE'S CALLED PUDGY!
IT SOUNDS LESS LIKE A DOG, AND IT SUITS HIM BETTER. HAVE YOU SEEN HOW HE'S GROWN?
YEAH, HE MUST WEIGH TWICE AS MUCH AS GRAPEFRUIT!
MROWWW!!!
UH-OH, YOU'LL HAVE TO EXCUSE ME. I HAVE AN APPOINTMENT AT THE VET! I GOTTA GO...
NO PROBLEM, I'LL SEE YOU TONIGHT AT CAMILLE'S.
REALLY, GRAPEFRUIT, I'M TELLING YOU, IT'S JUST A TINY POKE, NOTHING AT ALL!
?
RAF!
FETCH, PUDGY...! GO FIND THE LITTLE BONE!
?
POOR ERIKA, SHE STILL HAS A WAYS TO GO!

YOU SEE HOW CURIOUS HE IS?
CURIOUS? I'D SAY HE'S ANNOYED!

HIM AND TRAINS, THEY DON'T GET ALONG!
MROWW

OH!

BONK
MEOOOW

HSSS
HSSS

POF
MROW...?!

YOU SEE, TRASH-TALKER, GRAPEFRUIT LOOOVES THE TRAIN...
BEST FRIENDS FOREVER!

STRANGER THAN "DRACULA"!...
MORE FANTASTIC THAN "FRANKENSTEIN"!...
MORE MYSTERIOUS THAN "THE INVISIBLE MAN"!...

"THE MUMMY"!!!!
AAAAAHHHHH

GIRLS, ARE YOU...ARE YOU *SURE* IT'S A GOOD IDEA TO WATCH THIS MOVIE...?
IS IT DEAD OR ALIVE?
HUMAN OR INHUMAN?

ETERNAL PUNISHMENT FOR ANYONE WHO OPENS THIS CASKET!
MROWWW

"THE MUMMY"!!!
AAAAAHHHH

NO WAY! SORRY, BUT YOU'RE WATCHING THIS WITHOUT ME!
HEE HEE HEE!

WATCH YOUR EYES, I'M TURNING THE LIGHTS BACK ON!

CLIC

AMONG MAMMALS, THE CLAWS THAT GROW AT THE ENDS OF THE TOES ALLOW FOR SCRATCHING, SEIZING, OR DEFENDING. THEY ARE MADE OF ALPHA-KERATIN, AND THEIR LENGTH VARIES ACCORDING TO THE SPECIES.

IN SOME SPECIES, THE CLAWS ARE RETRACTABLE, WHICH MEANS THE ANIMAL CAN PULL THEM IN. FELINES, FOR EXAMPLE, HAVE THIS ABILITY.
FELINES? A CAT'S A FELINE, OR DO I HAVE THAT WRONG?
THE CAT IS A FELINE, ERIKA! NO, YOU'RE NOT WRONG!

WHAT?! BUT PUDGY DOESN'T HAVE CLAWS!
WHAT DO YOU MEAN, HE DOESN'T HAVE CLAWS?
ALL CATS HAVE CLAWS!

ARE YOU SURE?
ONE HUNDRED PERCENT! SCARE HIM, AND YOU'LL SEE...!

OKAY!
PUDGY, HEEL!

LET HIM BE! THERE'S ANOTHER WAY THAT'S TOTALLY FOOLPROOF.

OH YEAH? WHAT'S THAT?

WHY, YOU SIMPLY LOOK AT THE FURNITURE TO SEE IF HE'S SCRATCHED IT...!

HAPPY BIRTHDAY TO YOU! HAPPY BIRTHDAY TO YOU! HAPPY BIRTHDAY, DEAR PUUUUDGE...
MAOOWW
WHAT DO I DO? DO I BLOW FOR HIM?
MROOOOOW!!!
?! ...PUDGY!
SPLOOSH
SLURP!
YOU WERE SAYING, ERIKA?
OH, NOTHING, I THINK HE CAN MANAGE JUST FINE BY HIMSELF...

FROM LEFT TO RIGHT, PUDGY, IMNOPET, AND GRAPEFRUIT, A FEW DAYS AFTER ADOPTION...

FROM LEFT TO RIGHT, PUDGY, GRAPEFRUIT, AND IMNOPET, A FEW WEEKS AFTER ADOPTION...

FROM LEFT TO RIGHT, PUDGY, IMNOPET, AND GRAPEFRUIT, TODAY...

IT'S A GOOD PHOTO, BUT MAYBE WE COULD RETAKE IT VERTICALLY?
OH, BUT WHY? THIS PHOTO'S REALLY GOOD!
HMM...

PUDGY IS A GOOD CAT, FOR SURE. AFFECTIONATE AND MISCHIEVOUS, JUST AS HE SHOULD BE...
MEOW!

LAP
LAP
LAP
BUT WHEN IT COMES TO MICE, NOBODY WOULD SAY HE'S A FIRST-RATE HUNTER.

ACTUALLY, HE'S TOTALLY USELESS!

I'VE NEVER SEEN HIM CHASE A MOUSE...! ALL HE THINKS ABOUT IS FOOD!
NO SURPRISE HE'S OVERWEIGHT!

WELL, I'M GOING TO SET A TRAP. THAT WILL TAKE CARE OF THE MOUSE PROBLEM, AT LEAST.

ZZZ

CLAC!
MEOOOOWWWWW!!!
ZZZ...?!

NO COMMENT...!
MEOWOW...

A Warm Sweater

SORRY, GIRLS, I'M NOT GOING OUT...! I'M STAYING IN WITH IMNOPET!
IN THIS *BITING COLD*, HE'LL FREEZE HIS TAIL OFF...!

GRAPEFRUIT AND PUDGE, AT LEAST, DON'T HAVE A PROBLEM!
THAT'S THE ADVANTAGE OF BEING A FURBALL...!
OR A CHUB BALL...! ISN'T THAT RIGHT, PUDGY!

WHY DON'T YOU BUY HIM A SWEATER?
ALL THE DOGS HAVE THEM, THERE'S NO REASON HE CAN'T TOO!

A SWEATER...?

HEY, THAT'S NOT A BAD IDEA!
OKAY, GIRLS, IT'S SETTLED...

!?!

BRRR...I'M COOOOLD!!!

WELL, I THINK IMNOPET HAS SOLVED THE PROBLEM!

...BUT CAMILLE, YOU SHOULD THINK ABOUT PUTTING ON A NICE, WARM SWEATER!

Catsitting

POLLUX, WITH PIGTAILS LIKE THESE, YOU WILL BE THE QUEEN OF ANY BEAUTY PAGEANT!

AND AS A BOY, TO BOOT!

MAYBE IT WASN'T WORTH THE TROUBLE TO PAINT HIS NAILS...

RIIING

NOBODY MOVE, I'LL GET IT!

HELLO, TALK TO ME...!

WHAT?!

MRAOWW

IT'S LUCIE, SHE ISN'T GOING TO STAY AT THE BEACH TONIGHT AFTER ALL! SHE'S COMING TO PICK UP POLLUX IN LESS THAN HALF AN HOUR!

UH-OH, WHERE'S YOUR NAIL POLISH REMOVER?!

OW!

POLLUX, NO!

MEOW...

?!

PLOUF

THERE HE IS!
HOLD ON, POLLUX, WE'RE COMING!

MEOOOWWW!!!

POOR LITTLE THING! IF YOU ONLY KNEW WHAT A FRIGHT YOU GAVE US!
I DON'T KNOW WHAT THEY PUT IN THIS CREEK, BUT IT REALLY WORKS. DID YOU SEE HIS CLAWS?

WE'LL JUST DRY YOU OFF, AND YOU'LL BE FRESH AS A DAISY...
YEAH, WE NEED TO HURRY, LUCIE SHOULD BE HERE SOON.

THAT'S HER, I'LL GET THE DOOR!

HELLO, HELLO, I'M COMING!
JUST TRY TO HOLD HER FOR TWO MINUTES!...THIS RASCAL'S GOT SO MUCH HAIR!

HEY, IT'S NOT WORKING. LET'S TRY SETTING 2!

STILL NOTHING!
WE'RE DOOMED! DOOMED!

AND MEGA HOT, WHAT DOES THAT DO?

?!
?!

HI, MANON!
LUCIE, WHAT A NICE SURPRISE, WE DIDN'T EXPECT YOU SO EARLY...

BUT IT DOESN'T MATTER, WE'RE READY TO WELCOME YOU...

...I WOULD EVEN SAY WE ARE SUPER READY!
HA HA HA!
TWO MINUTES, I HAVE TO HOLD HER OFF FOR TWO MINUTES!

HA HA HA!
ARE YOU SURE EVERYTHING'S OKAY, MANON?

BUT OF COURSE, WHY DO YOU SAY THAT?

CAN I SEE POLLUX?

OH, WE TOOK GREAT CARE OF HIM, YOU'LL SEE. HE WAS A PRINCE.

WE EVEN GROOMED HIM A LITTLE...
?!

MEW?
ONE WORD AND I WILL MAKE YOU EAT YOUR HAIR DRYER!

IMMY, I HAVE A PRESENT FOR YOU!

LOOK, IT'S A MECHANICAL MOUSE!

I TURN THE KEY...
...LIKE THIS!

AND TA-DA... IT JUMPS!

MRRROWW
OOPS!

DON'T PANIC, CAMILLE, A CAT ALWAYS LANDS ON ITS FEET...!
BUT WHAT ABOUT FROM THIS HEIGHT?!

BOING

NO DOUBT ABOUT IT, IT NEVER HURTS TO LIVE ABOVE A PRODUCE SHOP!
FROM NOW ON, I'M EATING MORE BANANAS...

HELLO, MA'AM, I WOULD LIKE SOME CATSPIRIN, I'M NOT FELINE SO GOOD!
SORRY, GIRLS, I COULDN'T THINK OF ANYTHING ELSE...
Improv Comedy Contest
0
1
0
SKRATCH SKRATCH

≡NOM≡ ≡NOM!≡
≡CRUNCH≡
≡CRUNCH!≡
ZZZ...

CHE BELLA GIORNATA OGGI!!!

DID YOU SEE THAT, GRAPEFRUIT? I'VE BEEN WORKING ON MY ITALIAN!
CLASSY, HUH?

THAT MEANS, "WHAT A BEAUTIFUL DAY TODAY!"

DONE!!!
THUMP!

GET UP, GRAPEFRUIT, ARE YOU COMING JOGGING WITH ME?

MRROOWW!!!

FINE, SOURPUSS, DON'T GET MAD...I'LL LET YOU SLEEP!
I'LL GO WATCH SOME T.V.!

≡KLIK!≡
STARSKY AND HUTCH LALA LALALA LALA! STARSKY AND HUTCH!
ZZZ...?!

MRROOWW!!!
VA BENE, I'LL TURN IT OFF!

DO YOU FEEL LIKE GOING OUT...? I'M HEADING OVER TO CAMILLE'S TO EAT!

I GET THE IMPRESSION THAT YOU **DON'T** FEEL LIKE GOING OUT...
ZZZ...

WELL, I'LL GO WITHOUT YOU THEN. SEE YA LATER!

A FEW HOURS LATER...
JEEPERS...

...I'M POOPED!

SNNRRZZ PSHOOO...!
SNNRRZZ...!
PSHOOO...!

MEEEEOOW!
ZZZ...?!

SOMETIMES, I WONDER IF THE LIVES OF RESPECTABLE PEOPLE AND THOSE OF CATS ARE REALLY COMPATIBLE AT ALL...!

THE MYSTERY OF THE MISSING CATS!!!

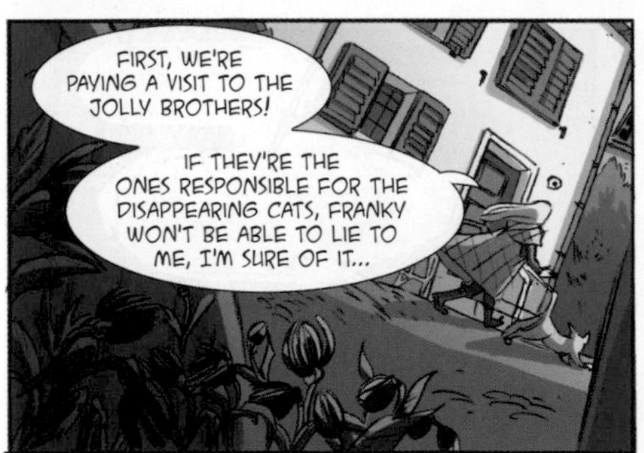

ALESSANDRO PÈTE 1 AN 04/11/07
HEH HEH... THIS SHOULD DO THE TRICK!

POLICE! PUT YOUR HANDS UP!
?!
CRACK!

I SEE WE'VE ARRIVED JUST IN TIME. DON'T MOVE, YOU'RE SURROUNDED!

FRANKY...THEY... THEY AREN'T JOKING...! THEY EVEN HAVE SERIOUS WEAPONS...! ASSAULT RIFLES!
DON'T...DON'T SHOOT...! WE...WE'LL TURN OURSELVES IN!

WHAT'S IN THOSE BOXES? CATS?!
WHAT? NO...! WE LIKE ANIMALS TOO MUCH TO GET MIXED UP IN CAT SMUGGLING!

IT...IT'S JUST PIRATED C.D.'S!
WE WON'T DO IT ANYMORE, WE PROMISE...

HMM...WE'D LIKE TO BELIEVE YOU. BUT WHAT CAN YOU TELL US ABOUT THE MISSING CATS?
IT...IT ISN'T US!
IF I WAS YOU, I'D GO CHECK OUT CRUDEVILLE!

WHAT-VILLE?
CRUDEVILLE...! IT'S THE TANNERY ON THE EDGE OF TOWN...!
THERE'S BEEN SOMETHING FISHY GOING ON OVER THERE FOR A WHILE.

WELLLL...WE'LL LET YOU GO THIS TIME, BUT DON'T LET US CATCH YOU DOING THIS AGAIN!
CROSS MY HEART AND HOPE TO DIE!

OKAY...CLOSE YOUR EYES AND COUNT TO A MILLION, GOT IT?
YEAH, YEAH, PERFECT!
MAY GOD BLESS YOU--YOU AND ALL THE OFFICERS OF THIS EARTH...!

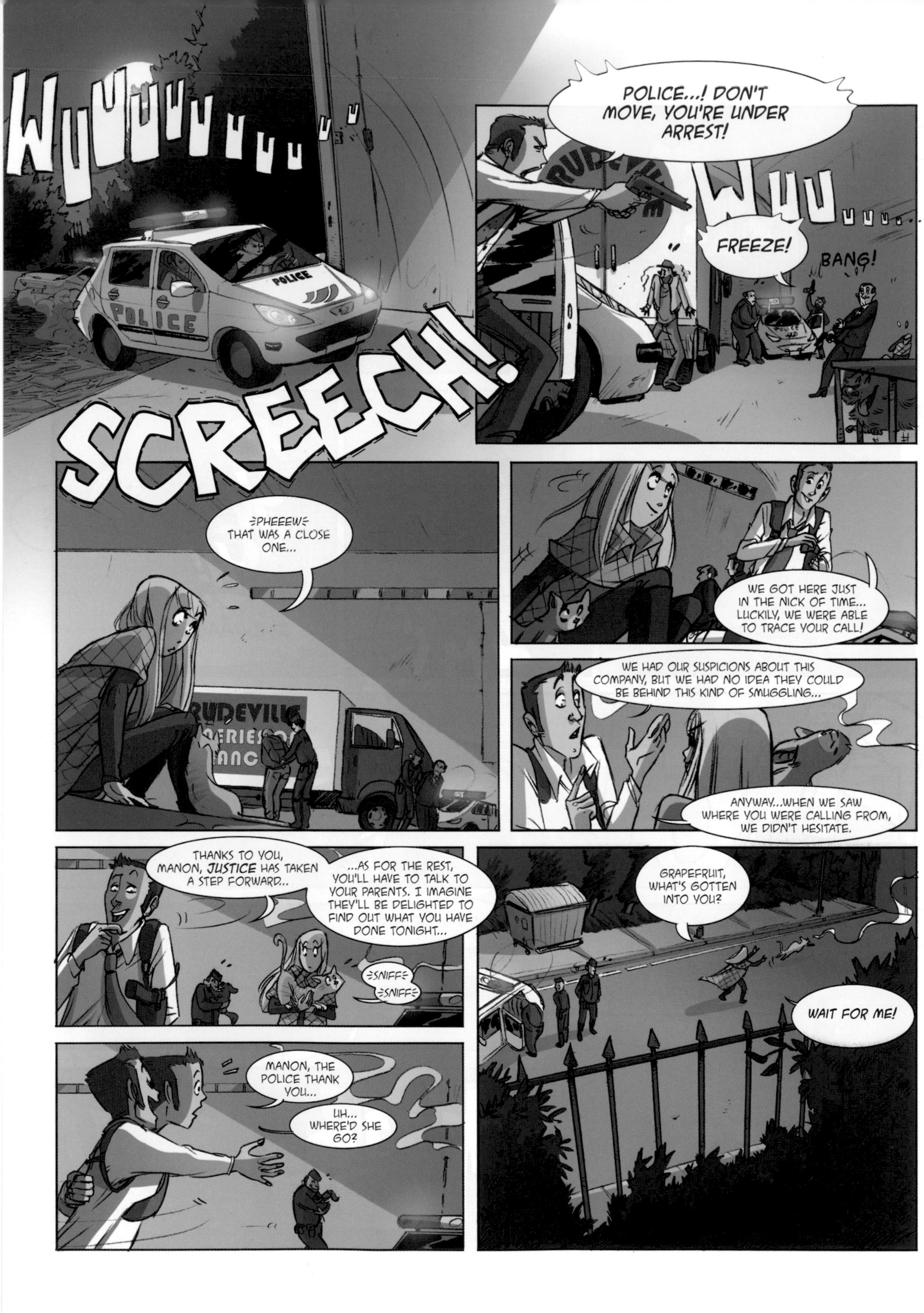

WUUUUUUUU
SCREECH!
POLICE...! DON'T MOVE, YOU'RE UNDER ARREST!
WUUUUUU...
FREEZE!
BANG!
=PHEEEW=
THAT WAS A CLOSE ONE...
WE GOT HERE JUST IN THE NICK OF TIME... LUCKILY, WE WERE ABLE TO TRACE YOUR CALL!

WE HAD OUR SUSPICIONS ABOUT THIS COMPANY, BUT WE HAD NO IDEA THEY COULD BE BEHIND THIS KIND OF SMUGGLING...
ANYWAY...WHEN WE SAW WHERE YOU WERE CALLING FROM, WE DIDN'T HESITATE.

THANKS TO YOU, MANON, JUSTICE HAS TAKEN A STEP FORWARD...
...AS FOR THE REST, YOU'LL HAVE TO TALK TO YOUR PARENTS. I IMAGINE THEY'LL BE DELIGHTED TO FIND OUT WHAT YOU HAVE DONE TONIGHT...
=SNIFF=
=SNIFF=

MANON, THE POLICE THANK YOU...
UH... WHERE'D SHE GO?

GRAPEFRUIT, WHAT'S GOTTEN INTO YOU?
WAIT FOR ME!

GRAPEFRUIT!

WEIRD, IT'S LIKE HE'S BEWITCHED...I DON'T LIKE IT.

STUPID CAT, HE'S GONNA GET ME KILLED!

POF

?!

AND THERE IT IS--THE MYSTERY IS SOLVED!
DEAR MS. LUCIENNE...! SHE'S SUCH A GOOD COOK THAT THE CATS JUST CAN'T RESIST!
MAOOWW!
MEW!
WELL, WELL, LOOKS LIKE WE HAVE ONE MORE GUEST THIS EVENING...!
SIT DOWN, LITTLE RASCAL, AND DON'T WORRY, THERE'S ENOUGH FOR YOU TOO!

ZZZ...!
RIIIING

UMM...HELLO...

=SNIF=
=SNIF...=
IT'S ON! PUDGY HAS FINALLY STARTED TO HUNT! HE IS REDEEMED!
YOU SIMPLY MUST COME!

SNIFF
SNIFF

HE SENSES SOMETHING! IT'S AMAZING!

PUDGY HAS THE FELINE INSTINCT! HE'S A BLOODTHIRSTY HUNTER!
I MEAN, DO YOU GET IT...?! A MOUSE IS GOING TO DIE!

AS TO WHETHER PUDGY IS A BLOODTHIRSTY HUNTER, I CAN'T SAY. BUT ONE THING'S FOR SURE, HE'S FAR FROM STUPID...!
WHAT DO YOU MEAN?

ME...? UH... NOTHING. JUST MAKING CONVER-SATION...
IT'S SETTLED, I'M CHANGING THE FLOUR!
NUM NUM

OKAY, I GET IT. I'M CALLING THE GIRLS, AND WE'RE GOING OUT.
AND THE FIRST ONE TO MENTION HER CAT BETTER WATCH OUT!
Today, I'm starting over again with my tenth diary!
I hope Grapefruit will have pity this time around...

A Nice Bath!

HEY, GRAPEFRUIT, DID YOU HAVE A GOOD WALK?

WELP, I'VE GOT A LITTLE THING TO TAKE CARE OF...
HERE, HAVE FUN WITH THIS!

GOOD, THAT SHOULD KEEP HIM BUSY FOR FIVE MINUTES...! ENOUGH TIME TO GET EVERYTHING READY...

...BEGINNING WITH THE STAR OF THE SHOW: A NICE BATH...!

PERFECT, I DON'T THINK HE HEARD A THING...
SILLY ME...I ALMOST FORGOT TO CLOSE THE WINDOW. THIS SCOUNDREL CAN'T HAVE A CHANCE TO MAKE A RUN FOR IT.
IT'S JUST YOU AND ME, GRAPEFRUIT!
MEOW?!
WELL, THIS ACT HAS GONE ON LONG ENOUGH. I'M JUST GOING TO HAVE TO TELL HIM...
GRAPEFRUIT, IT'S TIME FOR YOUR BATH!
MROWWW!!!
GRAPEFRUIT, COME ON, YOU AREN'T GOING TO MAKE A BIG SCENE OVER A TINY LITTLE BATH...! YOU'LL FEEL GOOD WHEN IT'S ALL OVER!

THAT'S IT, BADA BING, I GOTCHA!
SCRATCH!
WHAT? SCRATCH?! WHAT'S THAT SUPPOSED TO MEAN?
CRACK
AAAAAAH!
MEOOOWWW...
PLOF
ARGH!
GRAPEFRUIT, GET BACK HERE!
OOPS!

DING
DONG

HI, GRAPEFRUIT... IS MANON HERE?

MANON, ARE YOU HOOOME?

FRUSHH

WHY DOES IT LOOK LIKE A BATTLEFIELD IN HERE?

MANON?

I'M IN HERE!!!

IT'S NOT SUCH A BAD IDEA TO WASH YOUR CURTAINS, IT'S SOMETHING WE NEVER THINK ABOUT...
BUT REALLY, WHY DIDN'T YOU JUST TAKE THEM TO THE CLEANERS?
GRRR!

ZZZ...
GIRLS, I'VE BEEN STUDYING GRAPEFRUIT!

AT NIGHT, WHEN I GO TO BED, HE'S SLEEPING.

ZZZ...
ALL NIGHT... HE KEEPS SLEEPING...I'LL SPARE YOU THE WHOLE VIDEO OF THIS SCENE. IT'S ALMOST EIGHT HOURS LONG AND HE DOESN'T MOVE A SINGLE CLAW!

AND HERE'S A LITTLE IN-BETWEEN PHOTO!
WHEN I GET UP, WHETHER IT'S SEVEN A.M. OR NOON...

ANOTHER VIDEO! WHEN I'M IN CLASS...
YOU SEE THE INTENSE ACTIVITY OF MY CAT!

I GET HOME AND TAKE ANOTHER PHOTO... INCREDIBLY, GRAPEFRUIT'S STILL ASLEEP!

I GO TO BED, I GET UP...ALWAYS NOTHING!
WHADDYA SAY TO THAT? ISN'T GRAPEFRUIT SOME KIND OF SCIENTIFIC MYSTERY?
THIS HAS BEEN GOING ON FOR THREE DAYS!

IN ANY CASE, HE'S PURRING. THAT'S PROOF HE'S HAVING GOOD DREAMS...
PURR...
THERE'S NOTHING UNUSUAL ABOUT IT...! PUDGY ALSO SLEEPS ALL THE TIME, EVEN IF HE WAKES UP TO EAT A GOOD TWENTY TIMES A DAY...

Today's Special
Pizza
Ham & Cheese
SALAD ~ PIZZA
THE MOST HANDSOME OF ALL IS POLLUX, MY ANGORA CAT!

AND HIS LONG HAIR IS THE MOST BEAUTIFUL THING IN THE WORLD!

NO DOUBT, BUT YOU HAVE TO CUT IT SOMETIMES, RIGHT?
LIKE IN THE SUMMER, OR WHEN IT GETS MATTED...
NEVER! ONE MUST SUFFER FOR BEAUTY!

HEY, LUCIE, DID YOU SEE THIS AD?

LOOKING TO BUY ANGORA CAT HAIR BY THE POUND...
CAT WORLD

SO WHAT? YOU WON'T GET ME TO CHANGE MY MIND!

...WILL PAY TOP DOLLAR...

IT'S A GOOD THING YOU CAME...THIS WILL DO HIM A WORLD OF GOOD.
BZZZZ
HMPH!

I WON!!!
MEOW?

I KNEW CUTTING OUT THE PROOFS OF PURCHASE ON MY CORNFLAKES WASN'T A WASTE OF TIME.
OKAY, IT TOOK ME TWO YEARS...BUT SO WHAT?
RRR...

THEY DREW MY NAME, AND I WON A WEEK'S VACATION AT A RESORT IN CHINA!

...FOR TWO.

HMM...WHO COULD I BRING WITH ME?

MY BROTHER...? YUCK, I'VE GOT MY PRIDE!
GRANDMA...? OH SURE, WE'D HAVE A WILD TIME!

ERIKA...? ONLY TO HAVE CAMILLE SULKING ABOUT IT FOR THE NEXT TEN YEARS...
AND VICE VERSA!

MEOW!!!
WELL, WHY NOT? THE LETTER DOESN'T SPECIFY THAT IT HAS TO BE A HUMAN BEING...

PACK YOUR BAGS, GRAPEFRUIT, WE'RE LEAVING TOMORROW MORNING!

FETCH, PUDGY!

COME ON, BIG BOY, SHOW A LITTLE SPIRIT!

?

DOO-DOO-DOO DO-DO-DO-DO, DOO-DOO-DOO DO-DO-DO-DO... ...DO-DO-DO-DO!

HELLO, HELLO!

TO CHINA...?! WITH GRAPEFRUIT?!

BUT...SUCH A **LONG PLANE TRIP**...THAT COULD CAUSE **MASSIVE ANXIETY** FOR HIM!

REALLY?

HE COULD GET SICK...OR MAD...AND START HAVING "ACCIDENTS" IN THE HOUSE.

OH, **NO WAY!**

YUP. TRUST ME, I KNOW THESE THINGS.

I JUST DON'T KNOW WHAT TO DO. PUDGY STILL HASN'T CAUGHT A *SINGLE THING!*
I'VE TRIED EVERYTHING TO GET HIM TO HUNT...

OH YEAH? ARE YOU SURE?

JUST LOOK AT HIM. HE'S LIKE A LION ABOUT TO SPRING ON HIS PREY.

POOR MOUSE, I WOULDN'T WANT TO BE IN ITS PLACE!

MRAOOWW!!!

SEE, WHAT'D I TELL YOU?

A COMPUTER MOUSE...! I GUESS THAT'S A GOOD START!
WHAT CAN YOU DO, PUDGY'S A CAT OF THE TWENTY-FIRST CENTURY...
MRAOOWW!!!
HMPH...

tail
tail base
rump
hip
back
torso
scruff
ear
pinna
forehead
stop
muzzle
whiskers
chin
hindquarters
thigh
shoulder
chest
flank
abdomen
hind legs
front legs
4 digits
5 digits
paw pads
GOSH, DID YOU KNOW THERE WERE SO MANY THINGS IN THIS BIG BALL OF FUR?!

HA HA! YOUR PURSE OR YOUR LIFE, YOU OLD WINDBAG!

REALLY NOW, MR. BANDIT, I'M NOT OLD!

SHUT UP! MY SLINGSHOT IS LOADED-- NOW DO WHAT I SAY!

OH!

?

THE SIGN OF CATMAN! SHOOT!!

I NEVER GET A BREAK! BYE, SWEETHEART!

I'M OUTTA HERE!

STOP, THIEEEEEEF!

KITTY!
KITTY!
KITTY!
KITTY!

KITTY!
KITTY!
KITTY!
KITTY!
GLOM!
GLOM!

GLOM!
GLOM!
GLOM!
GLOM!
GLOM!
GLOM!

OKAY, KITTIES, THAT'LL DO!

OH NO, NOT HIM...

NOOOOOOO!!!

NOT YOU, CATMAN CAT, I'VE TOLD YOU A THOUSAND TIMES YOU'RE TOO BIG!
I'M NOT HE-MAN!

MEOW!
OKAY, YOU CAN COME...BUT YOU'RE WALKING!

GIVE UP, RATTER! YOU'RE TRAPPED LIKE A RAT!
NEVER, I'D RATHER DIE!

ZZZ...
GIRLS, IT'S OKAY TO BE ENTHUSIASTIC, BUT WE HAVE TO STOP BUYING EVERYTHING THAT'S ABOUT CATS!
ZZZ
YOU'RE RIGHT, THIS D.V.D. IS AWFUL!

THE MASKED BANDIT STRIKES AGAIN...! EIGHTEEN APARTMENTS IN TWENTY-FOUR HOURS! READ ALL ABOUT IT!!!
FACE TO FACE WITH THE MASKED BANDIT...! THE EYEWITNESS ACCOUNT BY THE SENATOR'S WIFE!
MENU
DAILY SPECIAL
• HERBED POTATOES
• EGGPLANT
• FRIES
• CHOICE OF DESSERT
12 EUROS
READ THE MORNING TRUMPET! ALL THE DETAILS ON THE MASKED BANDIT!!!

I KNEW IT, I SHOULD'VE GOTTEN A TIGER OR A PIT BULL...!
MEOW?

IF EVEN THE HOUSES WITH ALARM SYSTEMS GET BROKEN INTO, HOW IS AN OVERWEIGHT CAT GOING TO STOP THE MASKED BANDIT FROM ROBBING MY PARENTS' HOUSE?!

WHO KNOWS, THIS UGLY DUMP MIGHT BE HIDING A MASTERPIECE!

THAT'S IT, FAT CAT, DREAM SWEET DREAMS AND LET ME WORK IN PEACE!

?
SKRATCH
SKRATCH
SKRATCH

DANG, I FORGOT. I'M A... A...ALLERGIC TO CATS!

AAAT-CHOO

CRACK
ZZZ...?

THE BLOODY PATH OF THE MASKED BANDIT STOPPED BY A CAT...! HIS OWNER TELLS ALL!!!
IN THESE PAGES, THE RETELLING IN COMICS OF THE HEROIC BATTLE BETWEEN THE MASKED BANDIT AND PUDGY!!!
LOOK, IT'S THE CAT FROM THE NEWS!
MY GOOD-NESS...
ZZZ...
HEE HEE HEE!
MENU
SHOULD AGGRESSIVE CATS BE FIXED? THE COMPLETE FILE OF DR. MABUSE!
THAT'S RIGHT-- MOVE ALONG IF YOU VALUE YOUR LIFE!

THE MOST FANTASTIC THING ABOUT SUMMER IS THAT THERE'S NO SCHOOL...! TOO BAD THAT'S ALSO TRUE FOR MY BROTHER...
I'M HUNGRY!
I'M THIRSTY!
ARE WE THERE YET?

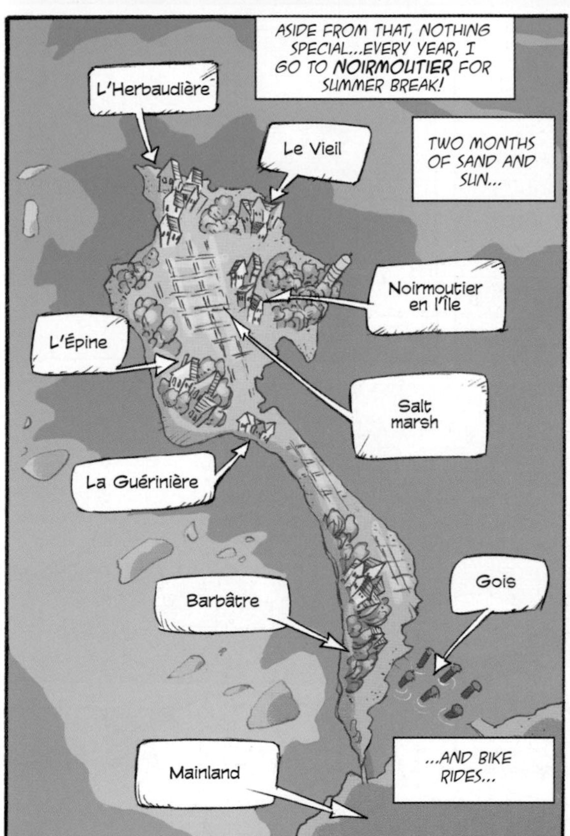
ASIDE FROM THAT, NOTHING SPECIAL...EVERY YEAR, I GO TO NOIRMOUTIER FOR SUMMER BREAK!
L'Herbaudière
Le Vieil
TWO MONTHS OF SAND AND SUN...
Noirmoutier en l'Île
L'Épine
Salt marsh
La Guérinière
Gois
Barbâtre
Mainland
...AND BIKE RIDES...

THESE TWO MONTHS ARE SO WONDERFUL, EVEN GRAPEFRUIT AGREES TO MAKE THE JOURNEY. POOR THING, HE HAS TO SPEND FOUR HOURS IN A CAGE...BUT, UNLIKE MOST CATS, HE TAKES IT IN STRIDE...
MRROWWW
WELL, KINDA...

I'M HUNGRY!
HERE!

I'M THIRSTY!
HERE!

I'M SICKA THIS!
WE GET TO NANTES IN AN HOUR, AND THEN WE TAKE THE BUS... LOOK AT THE SCENERY, IT'LL GO BY FASTER!

I WANNA WATCH T.V.!
ANYTHING ELSE?

IS IT MUCH LONGER?
NO!

WILL WE BE THERE SOON?
YES!

I WANT ICE CREAM!
...

I WANNA GO HOME!
GRRR!

MY GRANDPARENTS LIVE IN L'ÉPINE, THE MOST BEAUTIFUL VILLAGE ON THE ISLAND.
THERE THEY ARE...

MANON, WE'RE SO HAPPY TO SEE YOU!
HI, NANA! HI, POP-POP!
HI, GRAPEFRUIT!

BUT WHERE'S YOUR BROTHER?
THAT'S RIGHT, ISN'T HE WITH YOU?
OH YES... HE IS!
MEW!

...IN FACT, HE HAD A GREAT TRIP!

A Really Good Meal...

SORRY, GRAPESY, I'M AFRAID THIS CAN'T BE HELPED!
?
CAT

YOINK!
MROOWW

OH NO!
GOOD

GRAPEFRUIT, PLEASE, BE REASONABLE!

GRAPEFRUIT, HUSH!
MY LAME BROTHER WILL HEAR US!

MAOOWOOWW!!!

WHAT'S UP?
?!

HONEST, GRAPEFRUIT, I SWEAR I'D HAVE BOUGHT YOU DOZENS MORE LIKE THAT ONE...
SO WHERE'S MY PÂTÉ?
I'M NOT YOUR MAID!
SLURP
OD CAT

Long Live the Beach!

OH MAN, IT'S RAINING!

BUT WHEN IT RAINS, WE CAN GO RUN ON THE DUNES!
ZZZ...
NO, GRAPEFRUIT DOESN'T SEEM TO WANT TO GET HIS FEET WET.

...OR WE CAN GO TO THE POOL!
I'M KIDDING, GRAPEFRUIT...

...OR WE CAN CHECK OUT THE FISH AT THE AQUARIUM!

GRAPEFRUIT, I'VE GOT IT! WHADDYA SAY TO GOING TO THE BUTTERFLY GARDEN?!
ZZZ...?

HOW MUCH DOES IT COST?

FOR YOU, I CAN MAKE AN EXCEPTION --YOU CAN GO IN FOR FREE!
BUT ON ONE CONDITION...

...THAT YOU PUT YOUR MONSTER ON A LEASH!
I DON'T TRUST HIM!!!

MANON'S FAVORITE RECIPES
TODAY, GRAPEFRUIT'S CREPES!

GET A PAPER AND PENCIL, I WON'T REPEAT THIS!
MEOW!
CAT GRASS

WITHOUT A DOUBT, YOUR CAT IS DEVOTED TO THEIR DAILY PÂTÉ, BUT A LITTLE CHANGE WILL DO THEM A GREAT DEAL OF GOOD.
MEOW!
WHAT DID I TELL YOU?
CAT GRASS

THIS ISN'T COMPLICATED, YOU JUST NEED...
AN EGG!
A BIG PINCH OF CAT GRASS!
THREE AND A HALF OUNCES OF GROUND MEAT!
A HANDFUL OF ROLLED OATS!
THAT'S IT!

YOU CAN DO AN INSPECTION, GRAPESY, EVERYTHING IS FRESH!
SNIF
SNIF!
CAT GRASS

TO START, MIX ALL THE INGREDIENTS TOGETHER SO THEY FORM A LARGE BALL.
LIKE THIS!

NEXT, SPREAD THE MIXTURE OUT ON THE BOTTOM OF A PAN.
IT MAY BE CALLED A CREPE, BUT MAKE SURE IT ISN'T TOO THIN.

THEN PUT THE PAN IN THE OVEN. BROIL IT AT 400°F TO 475°F. FOUR OR FIVE MINUTES ON EACH SIDE, AS LONG AS IT TAKES FOR IT TO CRISP UP...
WATCH OUT, GRAPEFRUIT, YOU'RE GONNA BURN YOURSELF!

DING!
IT'S READY!
CAT GRASS

THERE, ALL WE DO NOW IS LET IT COOL DOWN.
MEOW!
YES, YOU HAVE TO, IT'S MORE DIGESTIBLE.
CAT GRASS

FINALLY, WHEN IT'S COOL ENOUGH, CUT IT INTO THIN SLICES.
NO, GRAPEFRUIT, YOU CAN'T HAVE ALL OF IT IN ONE GO!
CAT GRASS

LIKE THIS!

I'M HUNGRY!

HEH HEH HEH!

HERE YOU ARE, MASTER, IT'S REEEEADY!
?

HOP ON UP, WE'VE EARNED A LITTLE T.V.!
COOL, THIS ALIEN SHOW IS ON!
MEW?
IT'S ABOUT AN ALIEN WHO MOVES IN WITH A FAMILY! YOU WOULDN'T KNOW IT!
LONG BEFORE YOU WERE BORN, IT WAS ON T.V. A LOT!
WAIT, THERE ARE STILL THREE PAIRS OF UNDIES TO IRON...!
SMOOCH
YOU'LL SEE, IT'S SUPER FUNNY!
WHAT ARE YOU COOKING UP NOW?
THAT GUY, HE'S THE DAD. HE'S NICE, BUT HE'S KINDA OUT OF IT!
HA HA HA!
OH, PRETTY LITTLE KITTY!
I THINK I'M GONNA COOK A CAT!!!
?!
MAOOOOOOOOOO
OOPS, I FORGOT. THE ALIEN AND CATS AREN'T EXACTLY BESTIES!

The Adventure of the BLACK CAT

Well..."rest"...Given his antics, wild parties, and knife fights, it's hard to believe he was resting. But whatever, I report what they told me...if you're not satisfied, little diary, I'll close you and we won't talk about it again.

BOOM
BOOM
ALL ABOARD!
He was notoriously cruel! He sank every ship he came across...

YAIEE!
BANG
His enemies were terrified of him. With his cat on his shoulder, the Black Cat was a two-headed monster who could -- all at once -- shoot a pistol, cut off a head, and blind some poor fool with one slash of a claw.

MEOW!
BLACK CAT, IS IT TRUE WHAT THEY SAY? YOU DON'T KNOW HOW TO SWIM?
WHAT GOOD WOULD IT DO ME? THE ONE WHO CAN SINK MY SHIP HASN'T BEEN BORN YET!
The most surprising thing about this terrible scourge of the seas is that -- like more sailors than you'd think -- the Black Cat didn't know how to swim.

Hurricanes, whirlpools, and thunderstorms didn't scare him!
PLOSH
THE DEVIL HIMSELF COULDN'T GET ME IN THE WATER!
IF YOU SAY SO...

ZZZ...
MAN, THAT WAS SOME STUFFED CABBAGE.
HIC!
Then, one day, when he was distracted or had had too much to drink...

AH, I'M GONNA HAVE ME A LITTLE NAP.

MRRRAAOOWW
...?!
HSSS
HSSS
AAAAAAAAAH
PLOSH

Dear Diary, maybe you were expecting a more heroic death for such a formidable combatant, but what can I say? Sometimes reality is very disappointing.
I TOLD YOU ALL THIS TO CELEBRATE THE MEMORY OF A FRIEND OF CATS: THE BLACK CAT, THE FAMOUS PIRATE OF THE ISLAND OF NOIRMOUTIER.
NO DOUBT ABOUT IT, IT'S JUST A GREAT STORY...
HMM...
BUT...I ALMOST FORGOT! THE PIRATE'S CAT...?!
NANA, DO YOU KNOW WHAT BECAME OF THE BLACK CAT'S CAT?
NOPE.
Dear Diary, I'll leave you for now. But I'll be back soon to tell you about him...
ZZZ...

LITTLE MANON
Manon Hasn't Always Been
Tall and Beautiful

I'M NOT BOOTIFUL?

HAVE A GOOD DAY, MY LITTLE KITTY!

NO, MANON, YOU ARE NOT A FELINE! YOU'RE A HUMAN!

BUT...?! MY MOMMY ALWAYS TELLS ME I'M A KITTY!
LEAVES

MANON HASN'T ALWAYS HAD LONG BLOND HAIR...
LOUSY LICE!

ONE DAY, MANON GOT A LITTLE BROTHER...
I WANTED A SISTER!

SHE ALWAYS WANTED TO ADOPT A DOG, BUT THEN SHE MET GRAPEFRUIT...
MEW!

GOOD NIGHT, MY LITTLE MOUSE!
SMEK...
G'NIGHT, MOMMY!

NO, MANON, YOU ARE NOT A RODENT!
LEAVES

HAVE FUN, MY LITTLE DRAGONFLY, I'M WATCHING.
YEAAAH!!!!
ETC. ... ETC. ...

Dear Diary, I've always loved cats
My parents had one (who's still alive but much older now)...
Minos, when I was five...
Minos, today...
As you can see in this photo, I adored him!
I was also crazy about Jox, our border collie, who must be somewhere on an island paradise now...
Jox and me, then...
Jox, today...
But I digress...Anyway, I've always loved cats. I even thought I'd always behaved myself with them...
...until my mom found this old photo of me and Minos in an album...
...and this one, where my dad is telling me not to cut Minos's whiskers!
Dear Diary, if my brother finds these compromising photos, he could use them for blackmail...Erika and Camille absolutely must not find out about this!!!

THE ARCHIVES OF MINOS
MEOW!
Manon's parents' cat

NO, NO, AND NO! YOU WILL NOT CALL THIS CAT CLARA LOUISE!!!

THINK HOW EMBARRASSING IT WOULD BE IF YOU MET A PERSON WHO HAD THE SAME NAME...! IT WOULD BE LIKE THEY HAD THE NAME OF AN ANIMAL!

THEN, CAN I CALL HIM CLARINET?

CLARINET...?
HMM...
YES, IT'S NICE...! AND IT WORKS FOR A BOY OR A GIRL!

WHAT DO YOU THINK, LITTLE GIRL? YOU DON'T THINK SO?

SWEET LITTLE THING...SHE'S SO SHY.

CAT GOT YOUR TONGUE?
WHAT'S YOUR NAME?

CLARINET!
UH, WHAT IF WE CALLED HIM MINOS?

ZZZ...

ON YOUR FEET, FURBAG, WE'RE GOING FOR A LITTLE WALK!
MAAARROOW!!!

I'M GONNA SHOW YOU A SUPER-COOL SPOT!

THERE!

HOW ABOUT THAT? ISN'T IT NICE HERE?

THE ONLY ONES IN THE WORLD, WATCHING THE SUNSET!
DO YOU FEEL IT...? THE ONLY ONES IN THE WORLD!

DOO-DOO-DOO DO-DO-DO-DO, DOO-DOO-DOO DO-DO-DO-DO...
?

HELLO...? NO, OF COURSE THAT'S NOT A PROBLEM...

CLICK!
THAT WAS ERIKA. SHE'S COMING TO VISIT US TOMORROW...WITH PUDGY!

OH WELL, WE WOULDN'T HAVE BEEN ALONE FOR VERY LONG AS IT IS...
...AND ANYWAY, I WAS ASKING FOR IT! THAT'LL TEACH ME TO GO FOR A WALK WITH MY PHONE...
MEOW?
OF COURSE IT DOESN'T BOTHER ME...YOU'LL SEE, WE'RE GONNA HAVE LOTS OF FUN!

ERIKA SHOULD BE IN NANTES PRETTY SOON. I'M GONNA CALL HER TO MAKE SURE EVERYTHING'S OKAY!
MRROW!
TAP
TAP
TAP
BONG-BING, BING-BONG, BONG-BING, AH-AH, BONG-BING, BING-BONG...
THAT MUST BE MANON FREAKING OUT!
HELLO...! IS THAT YOU, MANON?
YEAH, YEAH, EVERYTHING'S FINE! WE'LL GET TO THE TRAIN STATION SOON, AND THEN WE'LL TAKE THE BUS TO NOIRMOUTIER!
DON'T WORRY!
PUDGY?
YEAH, HE'S FINE.
SURE, SURE, HE'S GOT NO PROBLEM TRAVELING!
YOU DIDN'T HAVE TOO MUCH TROUBLE GETTING HIM INTO HIS CARRIER?
HIS...CARRIER?
ARGH! MY HAAAAIR!
I HAD A FEELING I MUST HAVE FORGOTTEN SOMETHING...!
MEOOOOOWW!
DISGRACEFUL!

MANON, I'M HERE!
READ CAT WORLD

IT WAS A LONG TRIP, BUT SEEING THE WEATHER HERE, IT WAS WORTH IT!
EXIT
MEOW!

PUDGY!
OH!

OH NO, WE NEED TO DO SOMETHING QUICK! HE DOESN'T KNOW THE ISLAND--HE'LL GET LOST!
NO PROBLEM, I'VE GOT THE SITUATION UNDER CONTROL...

YOU'LL SEE, I HAVE ALL MY EMERGENCY SUPPLIES WITH ME.
A BOWL AND SOME MILK!

AND THAT'S IT. NOTHING TO DO BUT WAIT...

ASIDE FROM THAT, HOW'S IT GOIN'?
EXIT
THREE SECONDS MORE...
TWO SECONDS...
ONE...

THERE, WHAT'D I TELL YOU?
RIGHT ON TIME.

SPEED IT UP, PUDGY, WE'RE NOT SPENDING THE NIGHT HERE.
AS FOR YOU, THIS IS A WARNING NEVER TO PULL A TRICK LIKE THAT ON ME! UNDERSTAND?!
MEOW?
SLURP
SLURP!

OH, POOR LITTLE KITTY...! HE MUST HAVE BEEN ABANDONED, HE'S TERRIBLY THIN!
THIN...? BUT, MOM, DON'T YOU MEAN HE'S OBESE?
SHUT UP, YOU LOUT! GO FIND THIS POOR LITTLE CREATURE SOMETHING TO EAT!
YOWCH!
BOP!
AN HOUR LATER...
WHAT A SWEET PIGGY...! HE MUST HAVE BEEN HUNGRY!
ZZZ...
SLURP!
OH, THE LITTLE RASCAL...IT'S HIS WAY OF SAYING THANK YOU!
BURRRR
C'MON, WHEN I BURP, YOU BOP ME WITH YOUR CANE!
MEOW...
OH, YOU'RE LEAVING ALREADY...? COME BACK, LITTLE CAT! YOU'LL BE SO COLD AT NIGHT!
LOOK, THERE'S PUDGE...!
YOU WANNA BET HE CLEANS HIS PLATE BEFORE GRAPEFRUIT?
SLURP
SLURP
PUDGY
?!
PUDGY
ZZZ...
HOW MUCH IS THAT BET?
MRROWW!

Dear Diary, somewhere out there, there has to be one cat who is the biggest in the world. It stands to reason!
Z

There is also, without a doubt, the hairiest cat...

...and the dumbest cat...

But back to the biggest cat in the world...
ZZZ...?

MEOW!
...and his beautiful tenor voice.

In proportion to his weight, he eats the same amount as his peers.
SLURP!
SLURP!
SLURP!
SLURP!

He is also very energetic for a cat of his size.

The only problem is when he comes home...

AAAATCHOOO!!!
MEOW!
THAT LETS IN THE WORST DRAFTS!

Coq au Vin

The Big Leap!

IT'S SO NICE YOU CAME TO SEE US! GRAPEFRUIT AND PUDGY ARE HAVING FUN TOGETHER!
THAT'S TRUE, BUT I'M ONLY STAYING A FEW DAYS. I'M GOING TO BRUSSELS FOR A VACATION WITH MY PARENTS.

WE'RE GONNA VISIT THE COMICS MUSEUM AND BUY TONS OF COMICS!

THE MANNEKEN PIS FOUNTAIN...!
THE ATOMIUM MUSEUM!
SERIOUSLY, THEO, CAN YOU GO DOWN JUST ONCE?
BUS

THE GRAND PLACE!
WHAT GRAND PLACE?
THE GRAND PLACE! THE BIG SQUARE IN THE CENTER OF BRUSSELS!

BUT FIRST, PUDGY AND I WANTED TO COME TO THE ISLAND AND SAY HELLO!
...AND VISIT THE NOIRMOUTIER BUS STATION...!

WHY DID YOU WANT TO COME HERE? DON'T WE HAVE BETTER THINGS TO DO?

OH!
HEE HEE HEE!

MANON! ERIKA!
CAMILLE? WHAT THE...!

SURPRISE!!!

WEEELL, IT'S NOT EXACTLY A WINNER!
WHY ON EARTH WOULD THE JUDGES CHOOSE OUR CASTLE...?! IT TOTALLY SUCKS!
IT DOESN'T SUCK, IT'S JUST LESS...
LESS FANCY, LESS HIGH, LESS EVERYTHING... IT JUST SUCKS!
LESS...
I'M ALMOST ASHAMED TO BE HERE...
MAYBE, BUT WE HAVE A CARD UP OUR SLEEVE!
?!
GIRLS, I THINK I KNOW HOW WE MIGHT WIN THE CONTEST...
OH NO!
WHAT'S IT TO ME IF YOUR CASTLE WAS THE MOST BEAUTIFUL IN THE WORLD...?! I DON'T SEE ANYTHING BUT A PILE OF SAND!
WAAAAHHH!!!
AH, FINALLY...! HERE'S ONE THAT'S ENTIRELY ADEQUATE!
IF YOU WANT MY OPINION, IT'S NOT IN OUR BEST INTEREST TO LET ON THAT WE KNOW THOSE THREE TROUBLEMAKERS...
SKRATCH
SKRATCH SKRATCH

AFRAID OF DOGS, ME?! NEVER!
YOU DON'T KNOW ME VERY WELL, LITTLE LADY!

I TOOK A KUNG FU CLASS AT THE SHAOLIN TEMPLE...
WITH JUST ONE LOOK, THAT POOCH WILL KNOW WHO HE'S UP AGAINST.

HAVE NO FEAR, NO MUSCLEBOUND MUTT WILL PREVENT ME FROM DELIVERING THIS CERTIFIED LETTER TO HIS LORDSHIP!

ALL RIGHTY, BACK TO WORK!

MEOOW
YIPE!
HISS
SCRATCH
OUCH!

AAAGHH...! HELP, DO SOMETHING!
MREOWW!!!

HE'S RIGHT. I SHOULD DO SOMETHING...

THERE, THAT SHOULD DO IT...

WARNING
BEWARE OF
DOG CAT

SLURP!

HAVE YOU SEEN PUDGY?

PUDGY, WHERE ARE YOU?
PUUUUDGYYYY!!!
HERE, KITTY KITTY!

WAIT A SEC...THE LAST TIME I SAW HIM, HE WAS WITH ME WHEN...
WHEN...

WHEN I WENT TO GET THE ICE CREAM!
SHIVER SHIVER
MEOW...
YOU CAN COME OUT, YOU BIG GLUTTON!

DID YOU SEE THAT ONE? IS IT A COW?
WHOOOA!

AND THAT ONE, ISN'T IT A BRAZILIAN PARROT?
YOU THINK SO? I'D SAY AN ANDEAN PARAKEET!

OH, LOOK!
DON'T YOU THINK THERE'S SOMETHING FAMILIAR ABOUT THAT KITE?
OH YEAH? WHICH ONE?
UH-OH!

OH!!!

MEOOOW!!!!
GRAPEFRUIT!
GOOD OL' PUDGY, AT LEAST I KNOW YOU'RE IN NO DANGER...!
THE KITE WOULD NEVER GET OFF THE GROUND..

SKRATCH
SKRATCH
SKRATCH
THE GOIS IS AN ANCIENT ROUTE THAT CONNECTS THE ISLAND OF NOIRMOUTIER TO THE MAINLAND. IT'S UNCOVERED AT LOW TIDE.

IT'S IMPORTANT TO WATCH THE TIDE SCHEDULE, BECAUSE THE WATER RISES SUPER FAST!

SOMETIMES, PEOPLE WHO AREN'T PAYING ATTENTION GET CAUGHT IN THE TRAP! EVEN CARS GET WASHED AWAY IN THE WATER!
YIKES!

AND THESE POSTS ALL ALONG THE PATH--WHAT ARE THEY FOR?

AS A MATTER OF FACT, I WAS GETTING TO THAT...WHEN THE WATER RISES, IF SOMEONE DOESN'T HAVE TIME TO GET BACK ON SOLID GROUND, THEY CLIMB TO THE TOP OF A POST AND WAIT FOR HELP TO ARRIVE BY BOAT!

THE TOPS OF THE POSTS ARE ALWAYS ABOVE THE WATER! EVEN AT HIGH TIDE!

...BUT THAT'S SOMETHING I THINK OUR FRIENDS HAVE FIGURED OUT ALL BY THEM-SELVES!
HSS HSS
HA HA HA!

SNIFF
SNIFF
SNIFF
MEOW?

WOOF!

TELL ME, MANON, DO YOU THINK THERE'S A RISK OF **HEAT STROKE** OUT IN THIS SUN?
I THINK THERE IS IF YOU STAY OUT TOO LONG.
WHAT IF I TOLD YOU I SAW A CAT AND A DOG WHO WERE IN LOVE, THEY DUG UP A GOLDEN FLYING SAUCER RIGHT IN FRONT OF US, CLIMBED ABOARD, AND THEN TOOK OFF AND DISAPPEARED INTO SPACE?!
RIGHT, OKAY, WE'RE GOING IN...!

COME ON, GRAPEFRUIT, GET DOWN! YOU'RE GOING TO MAKE US LATE!
MRROW!!!

I PROMISE YOU WE'LL COME BACK SOON!
FOR SPRING BREAK, WE'LL STAY TWO WEEKS!

DON'T YOU WANT TO SEE PUDGY AND IMMY? YOU KNOW THEY'VE ALREADY GONE HOME! ALL THAT'S MISSING IS YOU!
HMPH!

THERE'S NOTHING TO BE DONE, HE REFUSES TO LISTEN TO ME!
MEOW!!!

WELL, WHAT IS IT, WHAT'S KEEPING YOU HERE?

?
?

ALL RIGHT, I THINK WE CAN GO!
SMOOCH!
MEOW!

A CAT IN A COMPLETELY NORMAL STATE. THE EARS ARE UPRIGHT, AND IT IS ATTENTIVE TO WHAT'S AROUND IT...
THIS CAT, WITH ITS EARS FLATTENED TO THE SIDE, IS NOT HAPPY, NOT HAPPY AT ALL...IT MAY BE AFRAID AND COULD EVEN BECOME AGGRESSIVE...
UH-OH, THIS CAT IS RAISING ITS TAIL IN ANGER. THINGS MIGHT GET OUT OF HAND HERE...!
THIS SITE IS A GOLD MINE...! TELL ME HOW THE CATS LOOK, AND I'LL TELL YOU IF THEY'RE IN A GOOD MOOD OR NOT.
DON'T WEAR YOURSELF OUT, THEY'RE SLEEPING...!
ZZZ

WHEN A CAT RUBS AGAINST A PERSON OR AN OBJECT, IT IS NOT SHOWING TENDERNESS BUT LEAVING ITS SCENT THERE--AND THUS TAKING POSSESSION...!
DO YOU BELIEVE THAT?
OF COURSE I BELIEVE IT. IT'S OBVIOUS!
I KNOW GRAPEFRUIT IS A VERY AFFECTIONATE CAT, BUT TO IMAGINE HE'S SHOWING TENDERNESS TO MY BROTHER, THAT'S QUITE A LEAP...
PTHBBBBT!

YOU'LL NEVER GUESS WHAT MY *FAVORITE ANIMAL* IS!!!
UH...IS THIS A TRICK...?

WELL, THAT'S IT, VACATION'S OVER!

IT'S THE RETURN TO NORMAL LIFE...TO MONOTONY!
PURRR...

MEW!
?

MEW!
MEOW!
MEW!
MEW!
MRREW!
MEW!
MEOW!
WHA...?! WHERE ARE ALL THESE KITTENS COMING FROM?

GRAPEFRUIT, DON'T TELL ME THAT YOU...YOU...
...YOU'RE THE FATHER?!!

MROOW!!!

MEOW!
MROOW!!!

HSSS
HSSS
...

OOF, THAT WAS A CLOSE CALL!
FOR A SECOND THERE I THOUGHT I WAS A GRANDMA!
PLOP!
PLOP!

...
SNIF
SNIF
...
...
...
...
I DON'T KNOW WHY, BUT THE CHILDREN AREN'T PLAYING IN THE SANDBOX THIS YEAR!
YES, I'VE BEEN WONDERING ABOUT THAT MYSELF...

Lady with a Kitty

After *Lady with an Ermine* by Leonardo da Vinci.

LIKE MANY CATS, GRAPEFRUIT HAS SURPRISING REACTIONS TO SOME THINGS...

AT THE SIGHT OF THE SMALLEST BLACK HOLE, HE CAN'T HELP IT --HE JUMPS IN HEADFIRST...
RRRR...
YOU OKAY, GRAPEFRUIT?

?

LIKE A BOX, FOR EXAMPLE...
GEEZ LOUISE...

GRAPEFRUIT, GET DOWN FROM THERE RIGHT NOW--AND PUT ALL MY SWEATERS BACK WHERE THEY BELONG!
HSSS!
A CLOSET FULL OF CLOTHES--WOOL OR COTTON, IT DOESN'T MATTER...

THE SOUP TUREEN THAT GRANDMA PASSED DOWN TO ME...
HAS ANYONE SEEN GRAPEFRUIT?
I THINK I HAVE...

ETC....
GRAPE-GRAPE, WHERE ARE YOU?

REALLY, IT'S NO BIG DEAL. I THINK IT'S FUNNY, BUT I TRY TO KEEP A STRAIGHT FACE AND ACT LIKE I DIDN'T SEE ANYTHING...
MEEOW!
HMM, I WONDER WHAT THAT IS?

...BUT ONCE IN A WHILE...LIKE THAT TIME WITH THE EXTRA-LARGE PAPER TOWEL ROLL, IN PARTICULAR...
MEOW!
ONE SECOND, GRAPESY... I'LL HELP YOU OUT, BUT FIRST I'VE GOTTA GET THE CAMERA, OR NOBODY WILL EVER BELIEVE ME...

AAAAH!!!

CAMILLE!!!
THERE'S A MOUSE IN THE HOUSE! WHAT DO I DO?!

WHAT DO YOU DO...?! SIC YOUR WILD BEAST ON IT! YOU'LL SEE--HE'LL TAKE CARE OF IT IN JUST ONE BITE!

PUDGY? I HOPE YOU'RE KIDDING. HE WOULDN'T HURT A DRAGONFLY!
MAYBE NOT A DRAGONFLY, BUT A MOUSE, THAT'S DIFFERENT...

FEED HIM HALF RATIONS, AND YOU'LL SEE HIS INSTINCTS KICK IN!
IF YOU SAY SO...
TONIGHT, HE'LL ONLY HAVE HALF A BOWL OF MILK... SKIM MILK.
?

MIDNIGHT--THE WITCHING HOUR...
PUDGE WAS SO HUNGRY! HE MUST'VE BEEN MERCILESS!
HEH HEH! THAT CAMILLE IS MACHIAVELLIAN...
THE WILD BEAST SLEEPS...AND JUSTICE IS SERVED...PROBABLY!
ZZZZ...

?!

ZZZ...
PRRRZZZ...
HELLO, MANON? I KNOW IT'S LATE, BUT I GOTTA TALK TO YOU...

I AGREE, THE DECORATING SCHEME IS PRETTY WEIRD...
Today we eat MICE!
ZZZ...
...BUT I SAID TO MYSELF, PUDGY HAS TO KNOW HIS ENEMY FIRST BEFORE HE CAN FIGHT HIM!

¡AY CARAMBA! I'M THIRSTY!
AFTER THIS DEATH MARCH, I CAN'T FEEL MY FEET ANYMORE!

MY FRIENDS, I THINK OUR HOUR HAS ARRIVED...
AMEN!
I CAN'T DIE LIKE THIS! NOT LIKE THIS!!!

OH, GIRLS, LOOK!
?!

OH!
WHADDYA THINK OF THAT?

WE'RE SAVED!
I KNEW IT! I KNEW IT!!!

AND A-ONE!
...AND A-TWO!

...AND A-THREE!

MEOW?

WHAT'S THIS, THE GENTLEMAN HAS FLEAS?
AREN'T YOU ASHAMED!
QUICK, IMNOPET, LET'S GET OUTTA HERE! HE COULD PASS THEM ON TO YOU...
SKRITCH
SKRITCH
SKRITCH

"KILLS THE FLEAS, LICE, TICKS, AND OTHER ANNOYING CRITTERS WHO MAKE LIFE IMPOSSIBLE FOR YOUR CAT!"
HMM... THIS OUGHTA DO IT...

BUT GRAPEFRUIT MUST NOT SUSPECT A THING!

HE'S SLEEPING. THIS IS THE MOMENT...
ZZZZ...

I SEE...I SEE...

NOT LIKE THIS! NOT LIKE THIS!
THE END OF THE WORLD! IT'S COMING!

LET US PRAY, MY SISTERS!
DONG

DONG
DONG
DONG
ZZZ...?!

OOPS!
?!

SHOOT, I ALMOST GOT 'IM!
MAOOOOO

ZZZZ!
SKRATCH
SKRATCH
SKRATCH
SKRATCH

I KNOW HE HATES THIS, BUT I HAVE TO HELP HIM IN SPITE OF HIMSELF...

HEH HEH! IT'S JUST YOU AND ME, YA OLD SCOUNDREL!

MAKE SURE HE DOESN'T WAKE UP THIS TIME!

DANGER ON THE STARBOARD SIDE...! SOUND A WARNING!

DONG DONG
TOOOOOOT
DING
ZZZ...?!

SKUNKED AGAIN!!!
MEEEOOOOW

¡AY CARAMBA! IT WORKED!
YES, THAT WAS A NARROW ESCAPE, BUT WE CAN'T GO ON LIKE THIS...
...WE NEED TO MAKE A PLAN!

I JUST DON'T KNOW WHAT TO DO ANYMORE!
I'VE TRIED EVERYTHING...!
SURPRISE ATTACKS, FOOD...
...A NEW MECHANICAL MOUSE HE HASN'T EVEN TOUCHED!
MRROW
IT'LL TAKE A MIRACLE TO GET RID OF THOSE FLEAS...!
HAVE YOU PACKED YOUR BAGS, GIRLS?
AND A-ONE!
AND A-TWO!
...AND A-THREE!
?
?
...OR A NICE BIG, APPETIZING DOG!

MROOWW!!!

BYE-BYE!
COCOA

I SWEAR, MANON! IMMY IS CONCENTRATING SO HARD, IT'S LIKE HE UNDERSTANDS EVERYTHING HAPPENING ON THE SCREEN!
IMMY...? YOU'RE KIDDING...

HSSS!
KIDDING...? NO, NOT AT ALL... THERE, RIGHT NOW HE'S CLAWING AT THE T.V.!

PAF

PTHBBT!

CAMILLE?

HMPH!
CAMILLE... ARE YOU THERE...?

ON OUR STAGE TONIGHT...
EVERYONE READY?
YES? THEN LET'S GET STARTED!

PRINCESS MANON
THE KING, HER FATHER
THE QUEEN, HER MOTHER
THE PRINCE OF LIGHT
THE PRINCE OF DARKNESS
THE DRAGONS
THE LITTLE DOG
THE PRINCESS'S CATS
GRRR!
THE PRINCE OF LIGHT AND THE PRINCE OF DARKNESS...! A PLAY BY ALIX PATAFIX AND FRED BRR, DIRECTED BY PAOLALA...

WITH JUST A BIT OF IMAGINATION, YOU GET THIS...

ONCE UPON A TIME, THERE WAS A VERY BEAUTIFUL AND VERY KIND PRINCESS WHO LIVED WITH HER CATS AND HER PARENTS, THE KING AND QUEEN, IN A MAJESTIC CASTLE...SHE WAS CALLED MANON.

THE PRINCESS LOVED THE PRINCE OF LIGHT, AND HE LOVED HER BACK, PASSIONATELY...

ONE DAY, THE PRINCE OF LIGHT DECLARED HIS GREAT LOVE FOR THE PRINCESS.
I LOVE YOU!
THE QUEEN WAS SO OVERCOME, SHE FAINTED DEAD AWAY...
HMPH!
OH, CUTE LI'L POOCHIE-POO...
GOOD, WELL, I'M GOING FISHING.
...AND THE KING SAID IT WAS FINE WITH HIM.

THE PRINCE OF LIGHT HAD A LITTLE DOG, OF WHOM MANON WAS ALSO FOND.
CRUNCH!
?
OW!
HE'S SUCH A GOOD BOY! GOOD LI'L POOCH...

NO, KIKI, WE'LL TELL YOU WHEN IT'S YOUR CUE. BUT RIGHT NOW, YOU NEED TO BE GOOD!
GRRR!
SNIF...

WHAT A GOOD BOY HE IS! A GOOD BOY FOR HIS DADDY!
SLUUURP!
ANYWAY, THIS VERY SWEET DOG LOVED THE PRINCESS JUST AS MUCH AS HIS MASTER, THE PRINCE OF LIGHT.

THE DAY OF THEIR WEDDING WAS SET FOR THE END OF THE HARVEST, BUT SADLY, AN UNFORESEEN EVENT WOULD PUT THE UNION IN DANGER.
A TELEGRAM FOR THE PRINCE!

THE DRAGON ARMY FROM THE ENDS OF THE EARTH HAD INVADED THE EASTERN EDGE OF THE KINGDOM...

THE PRINCE LEFT IMMEDIATELY TO DEFEND THE TERRITORY OF HIS FUTURE IN-LAWS AND ALL THE PEOPLE WHO LIVED THERE...

IT WAS A BAD SITUATION, BUT THERE WAS WORSE TO COME. A FEW MILES FROM THE PRINCESS'S CASTLE, THE PRINCE OF DARKNESS WAS WAITING FOR HIS MOMENT.
IF I FORCE THE PRINCESS TO BECOME MY WIFE, I WILL BE KING AFTER HER FATHER'S DEATH! HEH! HEH! HEH!
SQUEEK!

THE FIRST THING HE DID WAS KICK THE DOG, OUT OF PURE WICKEDNESS.
TREMBLE
BACK OFF, YOU FILTHY BEAST!
YIPE!
SHIVER

THE PUTRID FIGURE THEN PULLED THE PRINCESS'S HAIR AND DEMANDED HER HAND IN MARRIAGE.
NEVER!!!

BECAUSE SHE REFUSED TO MARRY ANYONE WHO WAS SUCH A VILLAIN, THE PRINCE OF DARKNESS THREW THE KING AND QUEEN INTO THE DUNGEONS.
BOO-HOO-HOO!
SQUEEK!
RESIST ALL YOU WANT, BUT YOU SHOULD KNOW YOUR PARENTS WON'T HAVE A MORSEL TO EAT UNTIL OUR MARRIAGE DAY!
HA! HA! HA!
HMPH!
MREOW!
HSSS
HSSS

HA! HA! HA!
SO BASICALLY, THINGS WEREN'T GOING GREAT AT THE CASTLE. MANON WOULDN'T BUDGE, BUT SINCE SHE LOVED HER PARENTS SO MUCH, THE PRINCE OF DARKNESS KNEW SHE WOULD EVENTUALLY GIVE IN.

HOWEVER, AN EVENT THAT AT FIRST SEEMED UNIMPORTANT WOULD CHANGE THINGS ENTIRELY. THE LITTLE DOG, WHO WAS FED UP WITH THIS ABUSE, MADE A BREAK FOR IT.
HA! HA! HA!
YIPE! YIPE! YIPE!

YIPE!
YIPE!
YIPE!

MEANWHILE, THE PRINCE OF LIGHT WAS OFF BATTLING THE DRAGONS, UNAWARE OF THIS TERRIBLE TRAGEDY...

...AND THE PRINCE OF DARKNESS CONTINUED TO BULLY EVERYONE AROUND HIM.
BOO-HOO-HOO!
HUR HUR HUR
UH-OH, LOOKS LIKE A STORM IS COMING!
MREOW!
HMPH!
HSSS
HSSS
INTERMISSION...

SO, WHAT DO YOU THINK?
IT'S NOT BAD, BUT TELL THIS DOG TO LEAVE ME ALONE...
GRRR!

End of part 1...

Banzai!

MEOW?
NO!

MEOW!
NO, PUDGY! IF I START GIVING YOU MY CORN FLAKES, YOU'LL GET TOO BIG!

THAT'S IT! TAKE A HIKE!

POOR LITTLE KITTY, HE'S SO DEFENSE-LESS...
IT BREAKS MY HEART.

BUT REALLY, HIS QUADRUPLE PORTIONS OF FOOD SHOULD BE ENOUGH!
ZZZ...

?

BOOM

DEFENSELESS?! THE THINGS I SAY SOMETIMES!!!
SLURP
LAP
LAP
LAP

I'VE TRIED EVERYTHING. PUDGY ALWAYS FINDS A WAY TO GET EXTRA FOOD!

AN HOUR AFTER HE KNOCKED OVER THE TABLE, I FOUND HIM GIVING HIS MOUSE FRIEND A BOOST SO SHE COULD OPEN THE CUPBOARD FOR HIM.
ZZZ...
ZZZ...

HE PESTERS THE NEIGHBORS UNTIL THEY GIVE HIM TREATS...AND IF THEY REFUSE, THEY BETTER WATCH OUT!

BUT...THAT'S EXTORTION!
YEAH, AND IT WORKS. HE'S GAINED EVEN MORE WEIGHT!

WELL, ANYWAY... HE'S ASLEEP. I SHOULD BE ABLE TO RELAX FOR NOW...

?!
ZZZ...?

ZZZ...

PUDGY!!!
SHHHHH...NO ONE'S EVER TOLD YOU NOT TO WAKE UP A SLEEPWALKER?

WHAT'D I TELL YOU...HE'S TERRIBLE!
ZZZ...

Do you remember, dear Diary, that I've been learning Italian?*
"CAT," IN ITALIAN, IS GATTO, AND "MOUSE," TOPO...
MEOW?
"MEOW"? THAT ONE I DON'T KNOW.
*We talked about this a few pages ago, too, if memory serves...

Okay, then let me tell you about Paola, my pen pal who lives in Sicily, in southern Italy.

...And about her cat, Camilla. She's a very nice cat, but if you want my opinion, pretty antisocial.
HSSS...
YIKES!!!
SHE'S SO AFFECTIONATE...
THAT'S HER WAY OF SAYING SHE LIKES YOU!

And a bit of a thief...

A big thief!
MY VEAL MILANESE!

MY CHICKEN NUGGETS!

MY OCTOPUS!

So, by the time she'd had Camilla for two years, Paola never got to eat anything anymore, and she was starting to get irritated...
I THINK I'VE GOT THE SOLUTION!

YOU WANT A LEEK?
HMPH...
In the end, Diary, Paola became a vegetarian, and ever since, Camilla has let her eat in peace.

BUT YOU DON'T EVEN KNOW! MY BROTHER'S IMPOSSIBLE!
FIRST OF ALL, HE DOESN'T SAY, "I **HURT** MY BACK!" BUT "I **HURTED** MY BACK!"...

HE SAYS "PASGHETTI" INSTEAD OF "SPAGHETTI," AND "FEBYERRY" INSTEAD OF "FEBRUARY"!
IT'S TRUE THAT "FEBYERRY" SOUNDS SILLY...

MANON!
?

HAVE YOU SAWED MOM AND DAD?
NOPE!

"HAVE YOU SAWED"...WHAT DO YOU SAY TO THAT ONE?

WHERE YOU'D SAY "LIBRARY," YOU CAN BE SURE HE'LL SAY--
"LIBERRY."
EXACTLY!

SO NOW YOU UNDERSTAND! IF I LEAVE GRAPEFRUIT WITH HIM, EVEN JUST FOR A WEEKEND, HE MIGHT TEACH HIM TO **MEOW** WRONG!

HAVE YOU SAWED CAMILLE?
NO! WE HAVEN'T ***SAWED*** HER...

MEOW!
I'M GLAD YOU LIKE IT, GRAPEFRUIT. I'M ALSO SWEPT OFF MY FEET BY THE BEAUTY OF THESE TREASURES!

?

MEWOW!!!
?!

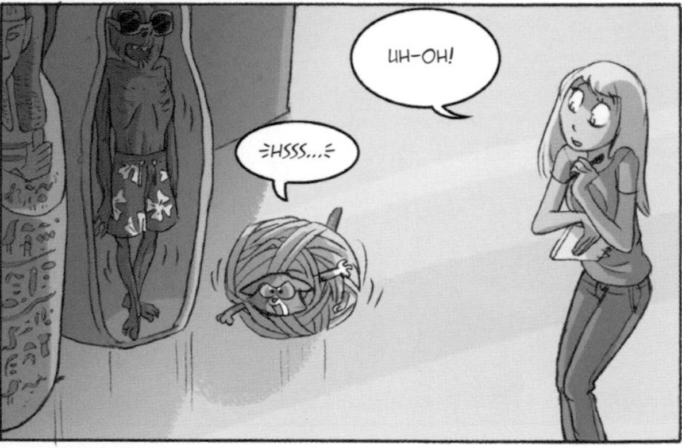
UH-OH!
HSSS...

PAF
MROW?
OUCH!
WHAT DID I SAY ABOUT BEING SWEPT OFF MY FEET?

I'M SURE THE ENGINEER WHO DESIGNED THE TRANSMISSION TOWER WAS A CAT LOVER!

Dear Diary,
They say cats and dogs are enemies...
That's totally wrong

Elephants are terrified of mice? I might buy that one. But this weekend, I went to my cousins' farm...

JOJO AND SIMON
CHANTAL
≡HIC!≡
COME 'N' EAT!!!
≡HIC!≡ HEH HEH...
RIKA
ESTELLE
NATHALIE
FRED
HA! HA! HA!

No, you're not dreaming... that is indeed a cat!

Dear Diary, I don't think I've told you about Spitfire, a super-cool big pony with a light-colored coat that my cousins ride sometimes to bring in the flock.
Well, today, they gave me a big responsibility: going to gather the ewes in a field at the other end of the farm. Can you believe it?
ALL SET!

And so we set off in single file--Spitfire, Rika, the cat, Grapefruit, and me...

...We'd gone one or two miles before we saw the flock of ewes in the distance.
THERE THEY ARE!

MEOOWWW!
?

WORN OUT ALREADY, GRAPE-GRAPE?
MEOOWWW...

I UNDERSTAND...! AFTER ALL, YOU'RE NOT USED TO LONG WALKS IN THE GREAT OUTDOORS.

OKAY, BACK IN THE SADDLE!

WOOF!
?
MROOW!!!

AWOOOOO...
OKAY...I GET IT!
?

Okay, so the operation was not a complete success, but you also couldn't say we returned empty handed...
CLUCK...
?
OH, I'M FINE!

Grapefruit loves life in the country...
Grapesy and the butterfly

CLUCK?
Birds he's never seen before...

Milk...
WHAT? HE DOESN'T WANT IT?
MOO?
IF IT'S NOT 1%, NOT A CHANCE!

Incredible hunting grounds full of mice...
SQUEE!

?
MROOW

A horde of mice...
SQUEE
SQUEE
SQUEE

MRROW?
YEP, GRAPESY, WE'RE LEAVING.
But all good things come to an end... Well, that's what they say, but I can still go back to the farm whenever I want.

My grandparents in Noirmoutier have asked me to join them on the island...
I don't know why exactly. They just said, "Manon, bring a magnifying glass, because you've got a case to solve!"

FÉLICETTE, THE FIRST CAT IN SPACE, OCTOBER 18, 1963

AT LAST, WE'RE FINALLY HERE!
MROOW!

MROOW!
QUIT WHINING, GRAPEFRUIT, I BET THERE'S A BANQUET WAITING FOR US!

HI, POP-POP! HI, NANA...! IT'S US!
WE'RE DYING OF HUNGER. IS THERE ANYTHING TO EAT?

?!
MEAWW!

HI, YOU!
MEAWW!

WHERE'D THIS KITTEN COME FROM?
WE DON'T KNOW.
THAT'S WHY WE CALLED YOU...SO YOU CAN FIND ITS OWNERS, IF IT HAS ANY.

YOU'RE SUCH AN EXPERT WITH THESE LITTLE CREATURES...
...PLUS, THEY'RE RUNNING A T.V. MARATHON OF ALL THE EPISODES OF NINE LIVES TO LIVE... WE DON'T HAVE TIME TO DEAL WITH THIS TOO!
ON THAT NOTE, IF YOU DON'T MIND...EPISODE 12,357 IS ABOUT TO START.

MEOW!
YES, I GUESS WE'LL FORGET THE BANQUET...A SAUCER OF MILK, HOW DOES THAT SOUND?

SWEETHEART, ARE YOU SURE OF WHAT YOU'RE SAYING?
YES, AZIZ, JEREMY WANTS TO BE CALLED MUFFY!
OKAY, MANON, DON'T START WATCHING, YOU COULD END UP LIKE THEM...

AZIZ, COME BACK!
NOT IF YOU CALL ME AZIZ! FROM NOW ON, I'M FLUFFY!

NOTHING LIKE A GOOD MEAL FOR MAKING NEW FRIENDS!

THE IMPORTANT THING IS NOT TO MAKE ANY SUDDEN MOVES--THAT COULD SCARE IT.
IT ISN'T RUNNING AWAY. THAT'S A GOOD SIGN ALREADY.
LAP
LAP LAP

MEAWW!
YOU SEE? IT'S PRACTICALLY EATING OUT OF OUR HANDS...

BZZZ
?

ACK!
MEEEW!!!

FINE, WE'LL GO WITH PLAN B...! WE TRAP THE BEAST, AND THEN WE'LL SEE!

MEAAW!!!
YOU SEE THAT? THE HARDEST PART'S DONE...

Dear Diary,
Do you know how Erika figured out Pudgy's gender?

It's very simple. She set out two cushions and put two comics next to them. One was "Lou!," a comics series about a girl, and the other was "Titeuf," a comic about a boy.

And since Pudgy picked "Titeuf," she deduced that he was male.
ZZZ...
I'm not sure that always works, but in Pudgy's case, somehow, it did.

HEY, KITTIES, I'M GOING FISHING WITH POP-POP...! KNOWING YOUR LOVE OF THE WATER, I'LL SEE YOU LATER!

MEOW!
?

COME ON OUT OF THERE, YOU SILLY!

MEWWW...
YOU TOO, KITTERS?

?

HSSS...

MEOW?
MEOW!

ANYONE ELSE IN THERE?

Once we'd gained the kitten's trust, we decided to go on a tour of the neighborhood in search of her owner...
LET'S START WITH THIS WOMAN.

EXCUSE ME, MA'AM, HAVE YOU MISPLACED A SMALL CAT?
BASEBALL BAT? NO, DEAR, I DON'T HAVE ANY NEED FOR ONE OF THOSE!

I'M ASKING, MA'AM, IF YOU'VE LOST A LITTLE KITTEN?
A TRIP TO BRITAIN? WHY, OF COURSE, I'D LOVE TO GO!

YOU WOULDN'T HAVE LOST A LITTLE CAT?
NO, SWEETIE! I'M SORRY!
NO, BUT COME IN IF YOU WANT SOME COCOA!
YOU WOULDN'T HAVE SEEN...
NO!
NOPE!
NUH-UH!

YOU...
NO!
NOPE!
NYET!
NON!
NEIN!

YOU KNOW WHAT, GRAPEFRUIT? THE ISLAND IS TOO BIG...
MEOW!

?

I THINK I HAVE AN IDEA!

A SMALL BLACK-AND-WHITE CAT HAS BEEN FOUND...! COME TO 24 RUE ST-JEAN IN L'ÉPINE OR CALL MANON AT 06-81-85-71...

POLICE
BUT REALLY... IT'S NOT...IT'S NOT... IT'S SIMPLY NOT POSSIBLE!!!

HAVE YOU EVER SEEN A YOUNG GIRL--A GIRL WHO APPEARS TO BE A COMPLETE INNOCENT --DRIVING WITHOUT A LICENSE BEFORE SHE HAS TURNED EIGHTEEN?!
THIS HAS NEVER BEEN SEEN ON THE ISLAND!
NO, NEVER, SO THEY SAY...

...AND WHAT'S MORE, AT THE WHEEL OF A STOLEN VEHICLE WITH A SCARY CLOWN ON TOP!
IT'S SIMPLY NOT POSSIBLE, AS I OFTEN SAY!

CAPTAIN, IT'S TRUE THAT THIS YOUNG GIRL HAS SINNED, BUT WITH THE INTENTION OF DOING GOOD.
AS FOR THE THEFT, CAN WE REALLY PUNISH HER FOR IT, KNOWING THE PANDER CIRCUS HAS WITHDRAWN ITS COMPLAINT?

FOR YOU, FATHER, IT'S EASY...! PARDONING IS YOUR JOB!
AND BESIDES, AS AN ISLAND CORRESPONDENT FOR THE WESTERN TRUMPET, YOU'LL BE ABLE TO WRITE A GOOD ARTICLE ABOUT IT!

I'M NOT DENYING THAT, BUT--
THERE IS NO BUT! CAN YOU IMAGINE THE TROUBLE THE ISLAND WOULD BE IN IF SHE HAD CRASHED INTO A NUCLEAR POWER PLANT?!

BUT THERE'S NO POWER PLANT ON THE ISLAND!
THANK THE STARS! WE HAVE ENOUGH TOURISTS AS IT IS...

WELL, FINE...I'LL LET HER GO THIS TIME, BUT IT CAN'T HAPPEN AGAIN!
DON'T WORRY, SHE UNDERSTANDS HER LESSON--AND I'LL TAKE CARE TO SLIP A LITTLE WORD ABOUT THE PROFESSIONALISM OF YOUR FORCE INTO MY ARTICLE!

DRIVING WITHOUT A LICENSE IN ORDER TO RESCUE A CAT...?! MANON, WHAT IS THIS?!
I KNOW IT WAS A BIG MISTAKE...BUT YOU HAVE TO ADMIT THAT NOW, THERE CAN'T BE A SINGLE PERSON WHO DOESN'T KNOW I'M LOOKING FOR THE OWNERS OF THIS LITTLE FURBALL!

WHO KNOWS, MAYBE THE WITCH OF PRÉ COURT-TÊTE WILL BE ABLE TO TELL US MORE ABOUT THIS...

MEAAW!
YES, GRAPEFRUIT, THIS IS IT!

HMM...MY GRIMOIRE SAYS THAT TO FIND THE OWNERS OF A LITTLE CAT, YOU NEED...
...ONE OLD EGGSHELL FROM A SEAGULL!

I DROP IT IN MY POTION, LIKE THIS! AND I KEEP STIRRING!

...HALF THE TAIL OF A NUTRIA, POWDERED!
THERE!

SEVERAL OYSTER SHELLS AND A PEBBLE FROM THE PLAGE DES DAMES BEACH!
I ALWAYS HAVE THEM IN STOCK!

AND FINALLY...A KITTEN, IN ORDER TO SPEAK DIRECTLY TO ITS SOUL...
MEOW?!

A KITTEN...? ARE YOU SURE?
OF COURSE, IT MUST BE COOKED WITH EVERYTHING ELSE...IT SAYS SO IN MY GRIMOIRE!

OH COME ON, WHY ARE YOU LEAVING LIKE THAT...?! IT'S ALMOST DONE!

They say the beating
of a butterfly's wings
in the Amazon can
cause a tornado in
China.
It's what they call
chaos theory...

I don't know if that's true, but what I do know is that the beating of a swallow's wings can have enormous consequences. A case in point...

Kevin Bouchard, an all-star archery champion, trains in the marshes of Noirmoutier...
He may seem smug now, but he won't look so smart after he's lost an arrow.

GNNN...

?
FLAP
FLAP
DZONNG!

SWIK!
?

THOK!

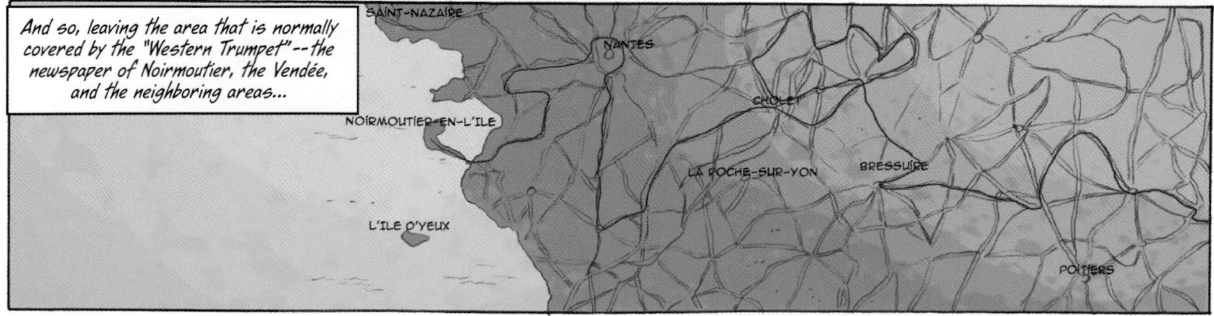
And so, leaving the area that is normally covered by the "Western Trumpet"--the newspaper of Noirmoutier, the Vendée, and the neighboring areas...
SAINT-NAZAIRE
NANTES
CHOLET
NOIRMOUTIER-EN-L'ILE
LA ROCHE-SUR-YON
BRESSUIRE
L'ILE D'YEUX
POITIERS

?

BRRAAK
WESTERN TRUMPET

?!

ANNA! THOMAS! COME SEE THIS!!!
TRUMPET

MEANWHILE, BACK ON NOIRMOUTIER...
SO, MANON, YOU HAVE ANY NEWS?
NO, STILL NOTHING...NOBODY'S CALLED YET.

DOODLE-LE-DOO, DOODLE-LE-DOO, DOODLE...
OH!

HELLO, MANON SPEAKING...

REALLY?! THAT'S WONDERFUL!

I'VE LOOKED FOR YOU EVERYWHERE, YOU KNOW! WHERE DO YOU LIVE?
IN CAMOMILLE-LES-BAINS, ALMOST TWO HUNDRED MILES FROM NOIRMOUTIER. DO YOU KNOW IT?

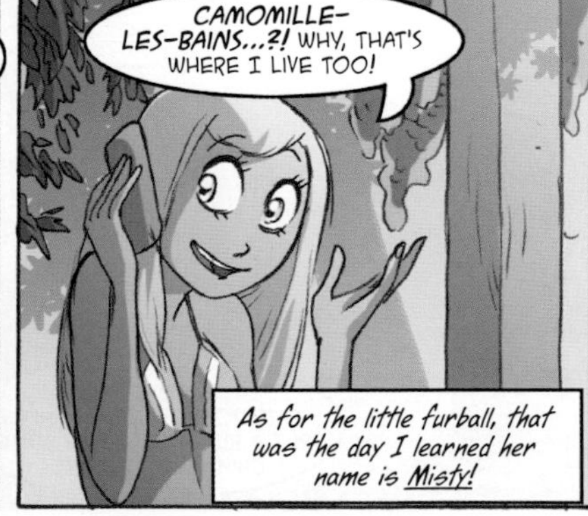
CAMOMILLE-LES-BAINS...?! WHY, THAT'S WHERE I LIVE TOO!
As for the little furball, that was the day I learned her name is Misty!

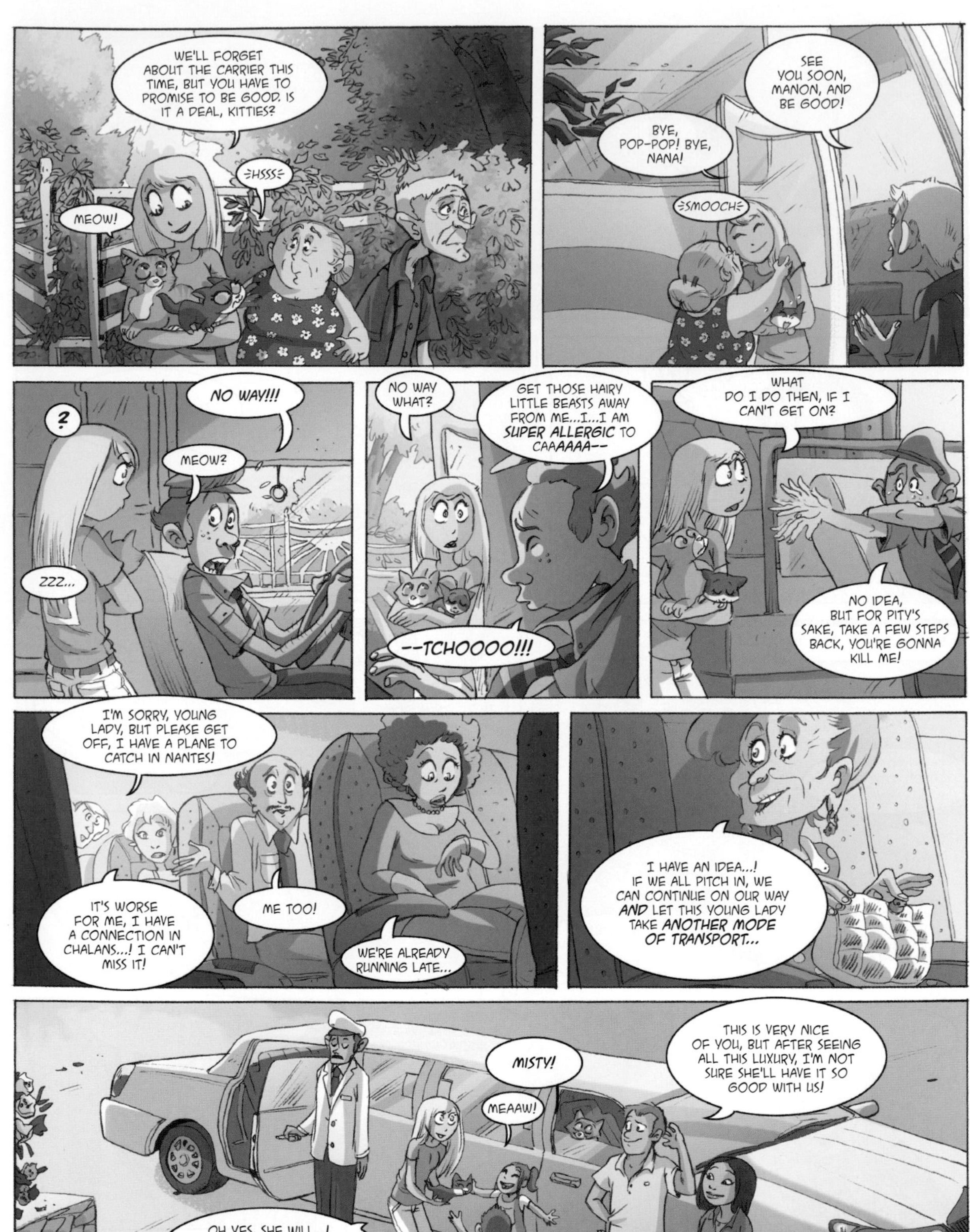
WE'LL FORGET ABOUT THE CARRIER THIS TIME, BUT YOU HAVE TO PROMISE TO BE GOOD. IS IT A DEAL, KITTIES?
MEOW!
HSSS
SEE YOU SOON, MANON, AND BE GOOD!
BYE, POP-POP! BYE, NANA!
SMOOCH
NO WAY!!!
?
MEOW?
ZZZ...
NO WAY WHAT?
GET THOSE HAIRY LITTLE BEASTS AWAY FROM ME...I...I AM SUPER ALLERGIC TO CAAAAAA--
--TCHOOOO!!!
WHAT DO I DO THEN, IF I CAN'T GET ON?
NO IDEA, BUT FOR PITY'S SAKE, TAKE A FEW STEPS BACK, YOU'RE GONNA KILL ME!
I'M SORRY, YOUNG LADY, BUT PLEASE GET OFF, I HAVE A PLANE TO CATCH IN NANTES!
IT'S WORSE FOR ME, I HAVE A CONNECTION IN CHALANS...! I CAN'T MISS IT!
ME TOO!
WE'RE ALREADY RUNNING LATE...
I HAVE AN IDEA...! IF WE ALL PITCH IN, WE CAN CONTINUE ON OUR WAY AND LET THIS YOUNG LADY TAKE ANOTHER MODE OF TRANSPORT...
MISTY!
MEAAW!
THIS IS VERY NICE OF YOU, BUT AFTER SEEING ALL THIS LUXURY, I'M NOT SURE SHE'LL HAVE IT SO GOOD WITH US!
OH YES, SHE WILL...! CATS DON'T NEED ANYTHING BUT A BIT OF MILK AND SOME CUDDLES, THAT'S ALL!

LOOK HOW SWEET THEY ARE!
MATH
?
MATH
WOW, WHO WOULD'VE THOUGHT PUDGY WEIGHS LESS THAN IMNOPET?
MAYBE I SHOULD TAKE HIM OFF HIS DIET!
OH MAN, I SHOULD HAVE KNOWN...
20 LB

HEY, LISTEN TO THIS--THE BUTCHER'S FILED A POLICE REPORT.
OH YEAH, WHY?
HE WAS ROBBED BY ***SAUSAGE THIEVES!***

NOW, WHERE WERE WE?
MRROW!
OH YEAH, THAT'S RIGHT.
The Prince of Light and the Prince of Darkness
Part 2

FSSSH
MEANWHILE, THE PRINCE OF LIGHT WAS OFF BATTLING THE DRAGONS, UNAWARE OF THIS TERRIBLE TRAGEDY...

AT THE END OF HIS MAD DASH, THE LITTLE DOG FOUND HIS MASTER.
YIP! YIP! YIP!
KIKI? WHAT ARE YOU DOING HERE?

ARF! ARF! ARF!
YOU...YOU WANNA PLAY FETCH?
LI'L BIG BOY MISSES HIS DADDY!

YOU WANNA FIGHT THE DRAGONS WITH ME?
ARF! ARF!
TO BE HONEST, I DON'T KNOW IF THAT'S A GOOD IDEA!

ARF! ARF!
HMM...NO, I DON'T THINK THAT'S IT...

WE NEED A TIME-OUT!

PATIENTLY, THE LITTLE DOG MANAGED TO EXPLAIN TO HIS MASTER THE TERRIBLE DANGER THE KINGDOM WAS IN...
THE PRINCE OF DARKNESS?! BUT...BUT THERE ISN'T A MOMENT TO LOSE!!!

ARF!
ARF!

MEANWHILE, IN THE CASTLE'S ROYAL CHAPEL...
MY GOOD FRIENDS, WE HAVE GATHERED HERE TODAY, IN THE PRESENCE OF GOD AND OF THIS ASSEMBLY, TO UNITE THIS MAN AND THIS WOMAN IN HOLY MATRIMONY...
...IT SEEMED PRINCESS MANON HAD GIVEN IN TO THE PRINCE OF DARKNESS'S THREATS.

HEH! HEH!
SNIF...SNIF...
MEOW!
ZZZ...
SNRKKKT!
HSSS!
HSSS!

...BUT BEFORE THE EXCHANGE OF VOWS, AS IS THE CUSTOM, IS THERE ANYONE HERE WHO IS AGAINST THIS UNION?
HSSS! HSSS!
...A HUMAN, I MEAN.

I AM!!!
?
?
SNIF?

I AM AGAINST THIS UNION, WHICH IS NOT THE PRODUCT OF LOVE, BUT OF THE DECEIT AND THREATS OF A VILLAINOUS, SCHEMING SNEAK!

EN GARDE!

THE TWO PRINCES CROSSED SWORDS FOR MANY HOURS, UNTIL THE MOMENT WHEN...
CLANG!
CLANG!

EEE! EEE! EEE!

...THE PRINCE OF DARKNESS TOOK THE UPPER HAND.

HA! HA! HA!
DIE, YOU WORTHLESS FOOL!

?!
CRUNCH

AAAAH!
KIKI?
GRRR

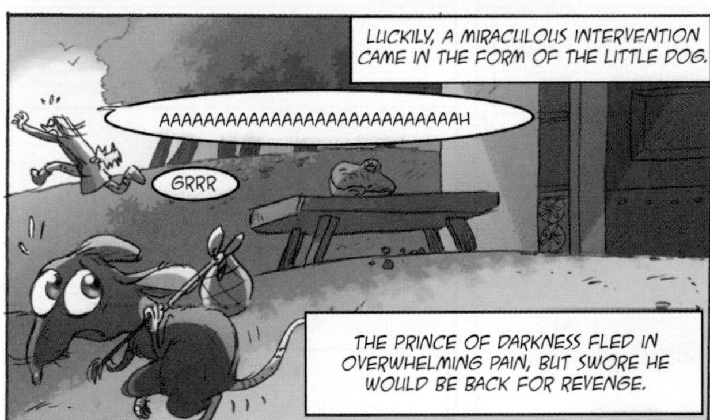
LUCKILY, A MIRACULOUS INTERVENTION CAME IN THE FORM OF THE LITTLE DOG.
AAAAAAAAAAAAAAAAAAAAAAAAAAAAAH
GRRR
THE PRINCE OF DARKNESS FLED IN OVERWHELMING PAIN, BUT SWORE HE WOULD BE BACK FOR REVENGE.

NOW THAT THE PRINCE OF DARKNESS WAS GONE, THE KING HAD AN IDEA...
OH!
WELL, SINCE EVERYTHING'S ALL SET UP AND THIS HAS ALREADY COST US A PRETTY PENNY, WE MIGHT AS WELL GET ON WITH IT!

ON THE SPOT, THE PRINCE OF LIGHT AND THE PRINCESS WERE MARRIED...

IT'S SAID THEY LIVED HAPPILY EVER AFTER AND HAD LOTS OF CATS...
EEP!
MEOW!
GRR
HEY, TELL HIM IF HE DOESN'T LET GO, I'M GONNA SCREAM...
THE END

I'M NOT MAKING A HABIT OUT OF THIS OR ANYTHING... AND NOW FOR A NEW FEATURE.*
Cat Facts and Figures...
*THE AUTHORS WISH TO STATE THEY STILL HAVE LOTS OF IDEAS, AND THIS IS NOT SOMETHING MANON CAME UP WITH TO BAIL THEM OUT.

DO YOU KNOW THE GESTATION PERIOD OF A CAT?
NINE MONTHS?
NO, IT'S NINE WEEKS!

AS FOR MICE, ALL THEY NEED IS TWENTY-ONE DAYS.
NO WONDER THERE'S SO MANY!

BY CONTRAST, ELEPHANTS HAVE THE LONGEST GESTATION OF ALL MAMMALS--TWENTY TO TWENTY-TWO MONTHS.
WHAT'D I SAY? THERE ARE MORE MICE THAN ELEPHANTS.

ONE OF BRITAIN'S LONGEST-LIVING CATS WAS MISCHIEF, WHO LIVED TO BLOW OUT THIRTY CANDLES.

"IN THE BOOK OF WORLD RECORDS, THE OLDEST CAT EVER WAS CREME PUFF, WHO LIVED THIRTY-EIGHT YEARS IN TEXAS..."
ZZZ...

"...I'VE ALSO HEARD TELL OF A CERTAIN BORIS, SAID TO BE OVER FIFTY YEARS OLD AND AGING GRACEFULLY ON THE ISLAND OF NOIRMOUTIER, WHERE HE ENJOYS A PEACEFUL RETIREMENT."
ZZZ...
"IT JUST GOES TO SHOW, YOU CAN GET PRETTY OLD BY SLEEPING A LOT."

AND WHAT ELSE...? OH YES, IF YOU ADOPT A CAT, TO WELCOME THEM HOME, REMEMBER TO GET A SCRATCHING POST SO THEY CAN TAKE CARE OF THEIR CLAWS.
EVEN IF, BETWEEN US, THEY'LL KNOW HOW TO GET BY JUST FINE WITHOUT ONE...

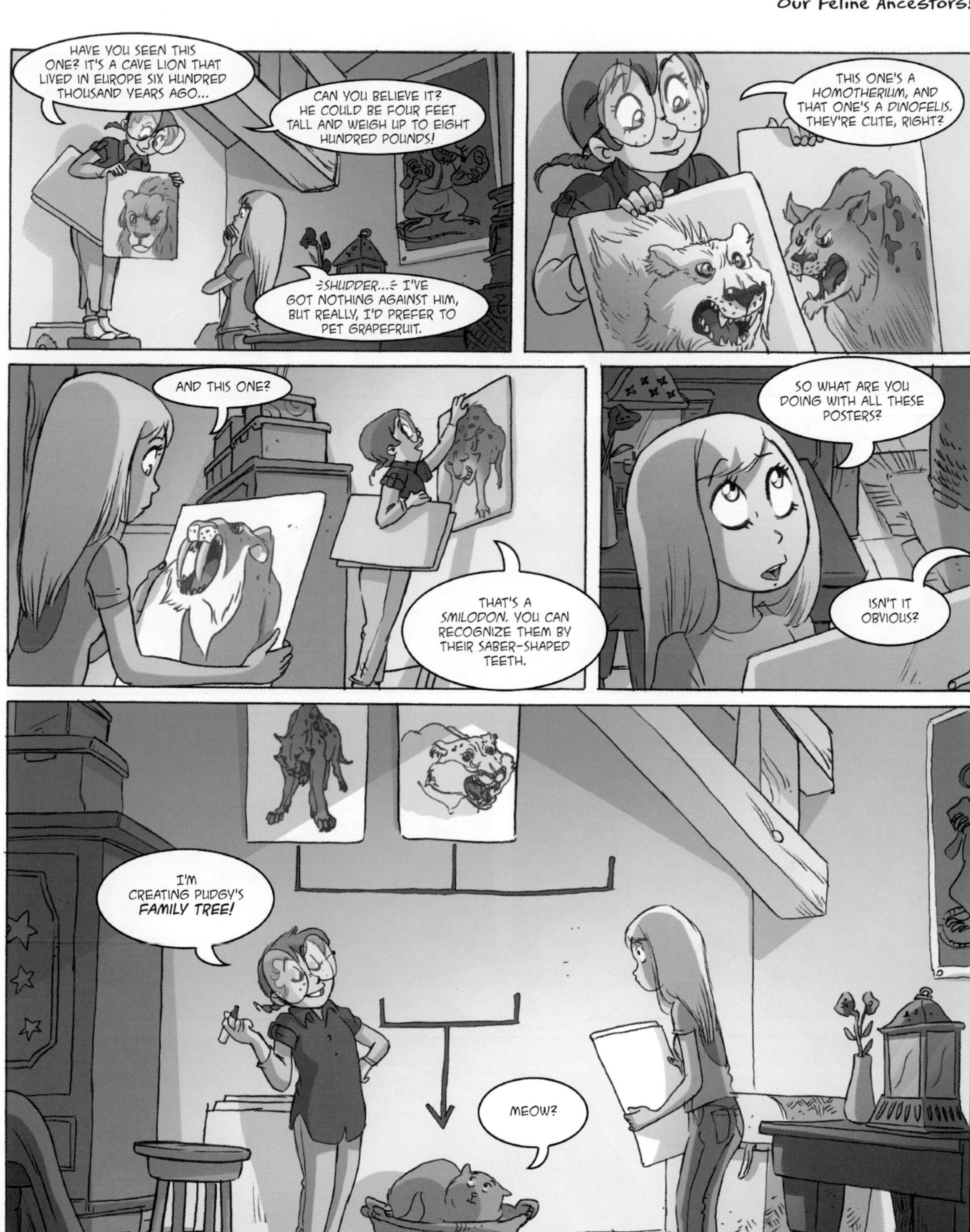
HAVE YOU SEEN THIS ONE? IT'S A CAVE LION THAT LIVED IN EUROPE SIX HUNDRED THOUSAND YEARS AGO...
CAN YOU BELIEVE IT? HE COULD BE FOUR FEET TALL AND WEIGH UP TO EIGHT HUNDRED POUNDS!
=SHUDDER...= I'VE GOT NOTHING AGAINST HIM, BUT REALLY, I'D PREFER TO PET GRAPEFRUIT.
THIS ONE'S A *HOMOTHERIUM*, AND THAT ONE'S A *DINOFELIS*. THEY'RE CUTE, RIGHT?
AND THIS ONE?
THAT'S A *SMILODON*. YOU CAN RECOGNIZE THEM BY THEIR SABER-SHAPED TEETH.
SO WHAT ARE YOU DOING WITH ALL THESE POSTERS?
ISN'T IT OBVIOUS?
I'M CREATING PUDGY'S **FAMILY TREE!**
MEOW?

POOR THINGS, WE CAN'T LET THEM GO ON LIKE THIS.
MROOW

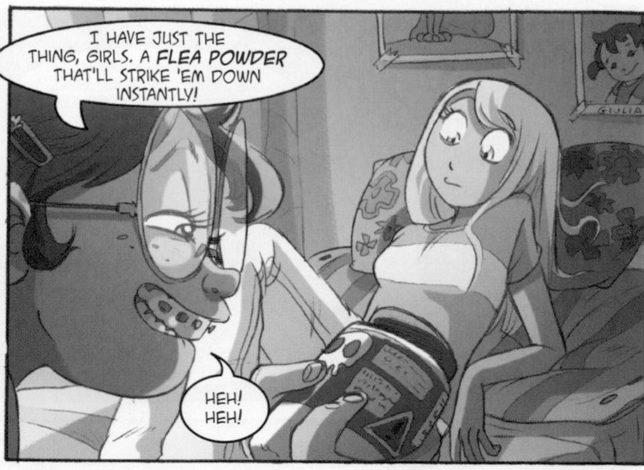
I HAVE JUST THE THING, GIRLS. A **FLEA POWDER** THAT'LL STRIKE 'EM DOWN INSTANTLY!
HEH! HEH!
GIULIA

I JUST THINK IT'S A LITTLE CRUEL. THE FLEAS HAVE A RIGHT TO LIVE TOO...
YOU HAVE A BETTER IDEA?

A FRIEND LET ME BORROW THIS *SPRAY.*

APPARENTLY, IT DOESN'T KILL THE FLEAS, THEY JUST RUN AWAY. IF YOU WANT, WE CAN TRY IT RIGHT NOW!

AFTER AN HOUR SPENT PERSUADING THE THREE CATS (OKAY, "PERSUADING," THAT'S A BIT OF A STRETCH!)...
MROOW
PSHH
PSHH

AND NOW, WE SHOULDN'T HAVE TO WAIT LONG TO SEE IF THIS STUFF WORKS!

YOU SEE, THEY AREN'T SCRATCHING ANYMORE! I TOLD YOU THIS WOULD TAKE CARE OF IT.

I WONDER WHERE THE FLEAS WENT!
TAKE A WILD GUESS!

IMNOPET IS THE PROUDEST CAT I KNOW. I ADORE HIM, BUT FRANKLY, WITH HIS SNOBBY ATTITUDE, YOU HAVE TO HANG IN THERE IF YOU WANT TO GET TO KNOW HIM...
ONE LITTLE KISS?
HMPH...

WHEN YOU PET GRAPEFRUIT, HE ROLLS ON HIS BACK RIGHT AWAY AND STARTS PURRING...
SKITCHY SKITCHY SKITCHY...
PURRRR...

WITH PUDGY, IT'S PRETTY MUCH THE SAME...AS LONG AS HE'S NOT EATING.
SKITCHY SKITCHY SKITCHY...
LAP
LAP
LAP

BUT AS FOR IMNOPET, HE MAKES IT CLEAR HE WANTS NOTHING TO DO WITH YOU...
SKITCHY SKITCHY...?
HMPH!

SOMETIMES HE ACTS LIKE HE DOESN'T EVEN SEE YOU...
HIYA, IMMY!
HE HAS A KNACK FOR MAKING YOU FEEL UNCOMFORTABLE.

BUT THIS MORNING, WHEN I WENT TO PICK UP CAMILLE, I GOT THE SURPRISE OF MY LIFE...
I JUST NEED FIVE MINUTES TO GET IMMY READY!
ARE YOU BRAIDING HIS HAIR? HEE HEE...

YOU KNOW WHAT? HE WAS TAKING A BATH, AND NOT ONLY THAT, HE LOVED IT--I'D SWEAR HE WAS SMILING.
?

I DUCKED BACK OUT QUICKLY. IF HE'D SEEN ME, I'M SURE HE'D HAVE ACTED ALL SNOOTY AGAIN.

PUSSES IN BOOTS

CREATOR BIOGRAPHIES

FRÉDÉRIC BRRÉMAUD was born in Seoul, South Korea, in 1973. After studying in La Rochelle, France, he joined the National Center for Comics in Angoulême. A prolific author, he writes comic books across many genres for readers around the world. Passionate about animals, he collaborated with the renowned artist Federico Bertolucci on the illustrated series *Love*, published in Europe and the United States. Also with Federico Bertolucci, he launched *Les petites histoires*, a children's series about discovering nature told through a combination of text, images, and comics (published in English as *Little Tails*). Frédéric is also the writer of, among others, *Lettres des animaux à ceux qui les prennent pour des bêtes* (*Letters from Animals*), with artist Giovanni Rigano, and *Chats!* (*Cats!*), with Paola Antista. He currently lives in Italy and on the island of Noirmoutier, France.

PAOLA ANTISTA was born in Sicily, Italy. There she studied foreign languages and literature; at the age of twenty-seven, she moved to Milan to attend the Disney Academy. Paola has worked as an illustrator for books published in Italy by Giunti, with *Un divano per dodici* (A sofa for twelve); Fabbri, with *Me, Mum & Mystery*; and Mondadori, with *Blanche*. At the same time, she began to work for the French comics market, publishing several comics series with writer Frédéric Brrémaud, like *Alix et Arsénou* (Alex and Arsénou) and *Chats!* (*Cats!*), among others. Recently, Paola has been the artist for Glénat's *Sorceline*, an ongoing series, and *L'île oubliée* (The forgotten island) for Jungle. In the United States she has worked for Dark Horse Comics and Disney on adaptations of *Dumbo* and *Frozen*.

EXECUTIVE VICE PRESIDENT **NEIL HANKERSON**

CHIEF FINANCIAL OFFICER **TOM WEDDLE**

VICE PRESIDENT OF PUBLISHING **RANDY STRADLEY**

CHIEF BUSINESS DEVELOPMENT OFFICER **NICK MCWHORTER**

CHIEF INFORMATION OFFICER **DALE LAFOUNTAIN**

VICE PRESIDENT OF MARKETING **MATT PARKINSON**

VICE PRESIDENT OF PRODUCTION AND SCHEDULING **VANESSA TODD-HOLMES**

VICE PRESIDENT OF BOOK TRADE AND DIGITAL SALES **MARK BERNARDI**

GENERAL COUNSEL **KEN LIZZI**

EDITOR IN CHIEF **DAVE MARSHALL**

EDITORIAL DIRECTOR **DAVEY ESTRADA**

SENIOR BOOKS EDITOR **CHRIS WARNER**

DIRECTOR OF SPECIALTY PROJECTS **CARY GRAZZINI**

ART DIRECTOR **LIA RIBACCHI**

DIRECTOR OF DIGITAL ART AND PREPRESS **MATT DRYER**

SENIOR DIRECTOR OF LICENSED PUBLICATIONS **MICHAEL GOMBOS**

DIRECTOR OF CUSTOM PROGRAMS **KARI YADRO**

DIRECTOR OF INTERNATIONAL LICENSING **KARI TORSON**

DIRECTOR OF TRADE SALES **SEAN BRICE**

ALSO AVAILABLE FROM DARK HORSE!

THE HIT VIDEO GAME CONTINUES ITS COMIC BOOK INVASION!

THE ART OF PLANTS VS. ZOMBIES
Part zombie memoir, part celebration of zombie triumphs, and part anti-plant screed, *The Art of Plants vs. Zombies* is a treasure trove of never-before-seen concept art, character sketches, and surprises from PopCap's popular *Plants vs. Zombies* games!
ISBN 978-1-61655-331-9 | $10.99

PLANTS VS. ZOMBIES: LAWNMAGEDDON
Crazy Dave—the babbling-yet-brilliant inventor and top-notch neighborhood defender—helps young adventurer Nate fend off a zombie invasion that threatens to overrun the peaceful town of Neighborville in *Plants vs. Zombies: Lawnmageddon*! Their only hope is a brave army of chomping, squashing, and pea-shooting plants! A wacky adventure for zombie zappers young and old!
ISBN 978-1-61655-192-6 | $10.99

PLANTS VS. ZOMBIES: TIMEPOCALYPSE
Crazy Dave helps Patrice and Nate Timely fend off Zomboss' latest attack in *Plants vs. Zombies: Timepocalypse*! This new standalone tale will tickle your funny bones and thrill your brains through any timeline!
ISBN 978-1-61655-621-1 | $10.99

PLANTS VS. ZOMBIES: BULLY FOR YOU
Patrice and Nate are ready to investigate a strange college campus to keep the streets safe from zombies!
ISBN 978-1-61655-889-5 | $10.99

PLANTS VS. ZOMBIES: GARDEN WARFARE VOLUME 1
Based on the hit video game, this comic tells the story leading up to the events in *Plants vs. Zombies: Garden Warfare 2*!
ISBN 978-1-61655-946-5 | $10.99

Volume 2 ISBN 978-1-50670-548-4 | $10.99

Volume 3 ISBN 978-1-50670-837-9 | $10.99

PLANTS VS. ZOMBIES: GROWN SWEET HOME
With newfound knowledge of humanity, Dr. Zomboss strikes at the heart of Neighborville . . . sparking a series of plant-versus-zombie brawls!
ISBN 978-1-61655-971-7 | $10.99

PLANTS VS. ZOMBIES: PETAL TO THE METAL
Crazy Dave takes on the tough *Don't Blink* video game—and challenges Dr. Zomboss to a race to determine the future of Neighborville!
ISBN 978-1-61655-999-1 | $10.99

PLANTS VS. ZOMBIES: BOOM BOOM MUSHROOM
The gang discover Zomboss' secret plan for swallowing the city of Neighborville whole! A rare mushroom must be found in order to save the humans aboveground!
ISBN 978-1-50670-037-3 | $10.99

PLANTS VS. ZOMBIES: BATTLE EXTRAVAGONZO
Zomboss is back, hoping to buy the same factory that Crazy Dave is eyeing! Will Crazy Dave and his intelligent plants beat Zomboss and his zombie army to the punch?
ISBN 978-1-50670-189-9 | $10.99

PLANTS VS. ZOMBIES: LAWN OF DOOM
With Zomboss filling everyone's yards with traps and special soldiers, will he and his zombie army turn Halloween into their zanier Lawn of Doom celebration?!
ISBN 978-1-50670-204-9 | $10.99

PLANTS VS. ZOMBIES: THE GREATEST SHOW UNEARTHED
Dr. Zomboss believes that all humans hold a secret desire to run away and join the circus, so he aims to use his "Big Z's Adequately Amazing Flytrap Circus" to lure Neighborville's citizens to their doom!
ISBN 978-1-50670-298-8 | $10.99

PLANTS VS. ZOMBIES: RUMBLE AT LAKE GUMBO
The battle for clean water begins! Nate, Patrice, and Crazy Dave spot trouble and grab all the Tangle Kelp and Party Crabs they can to quell another zombie attack!
ISBN 978-1-50670-497-5 | $10.99

PLANTS VS. ZOMBIES: WAR AND PEAS
When Dr. Zomboss and Crazy Dave find themselves members of the same book club, a literary war is inevitable! The position of leader of the book club opens up and Zomboss and Crazy Dave compete for the top spot in a scholarly scuffle for the ages!
ISBN 978-1-50670-677-1 | $10.99

PLANTS VS. ZOMBIES: DINO-MIGHT
Dr. Zomboss sets his sights on destroying the yards in town and rendering the plants homeless—and his plans include dogs, cats, rabbits, hammock sloths, and, somehow, dinosaurs . . . !
ISBN 978-1-50670-838-6 | $10.99

PLANTS VS. ZOMBIES: SNOW THANKS
Dr. Zomboss invents a Cold Crystal capable of freezing Neighborville, burying the town in snow and ice! It's up to the humans and the fieriest plants to save Neighborville—with the help of pirates!
ISBN 978-1-50670-839-3 | $10.99

PLANTS VS. ZOMBIES: A LITTLE PROBLEM
Will an invasion of teeny-tiny miniature zombies mean the party for Crazy Dave's two-hundred-year-old pants gets canceled?
ISBN 978-1-50670-840-9 | $10.99

PLANTS VS. ZOMBIES: BETTER HOMES AND GUARDENS
Nate and Patrice try thwarting zombie attacks by putting defending "Guardens" plants inside homes as well as in yards! But as soon as Dr. Zomboss finds out, he's determined to circumvent this plan with an epically evil one of his own . . .
ISBN 978-1-50671-305-2 | $10.99

PLANTS VS. ZOMBIES: MULTI-BALL-ISTIC
Dr. Zomboss turns the entirety of Neighborville into a giant, fully functional pinball machine! Nate, Patrice, and their plant posse must find a way to halt this uniquely horrifying zombie invasion. Will the battle go full-tilt zombies?!
ISBN 978-1-50671-307-6 | $10.99

PLANTS VS. ZOMBIES: CONSTRUCTIONARY TALES
A behind-the-scenes look at the secret schemes and craziest contraptions concocted by Zomboss, as he proudly leads around a film crew from the Zombie Broadcasting Network!
ISBN 978-1-50672-091-3 | $10.99

AVAILABLE AT YOUR LOCAL COMICS SHOP OR BOOKSTORE
To find a comics shop in your area, visit comicshoplocator.com. For more information or to order direct, visit **DarkHorse.com**

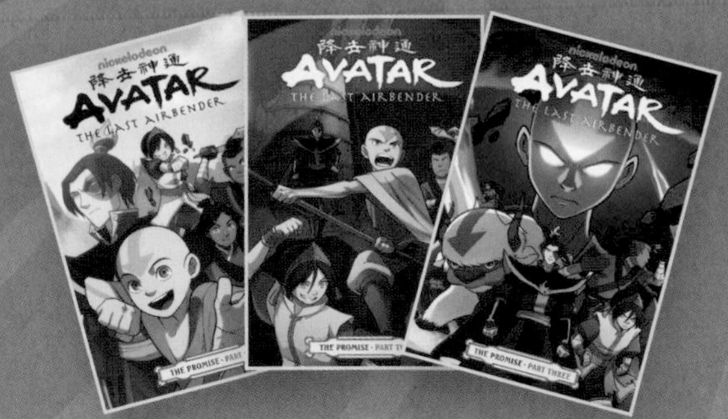

Avatar: The Last Airbender—The Promise Library Edition
978-1-61655-074-5 $39.99

Avatar: The Last Airbender—The Promise Part 1
978-1-59582-811-8 $12.99

Avatar: The Last Airbender—The Promise Part 2
978-1-59582-875-0 $12.99

Avatar: The Last Airbender—The Promise Part 3
978-1-59582-941-2 $12.99

Avatar: The Last Airbender—The Search Library Edition
978-1-61655-226-8 $39.99

Avatar: The Last Airbender—The Search Part 1
978-1-61655-054-7 $12.99

Avatar: The Last Airbender—The Search Part 2
978-1-61655-190-2 $12.99

Avatar: The Last Airbender—The Search Part 3
978-1-61655-184-1 $12.99

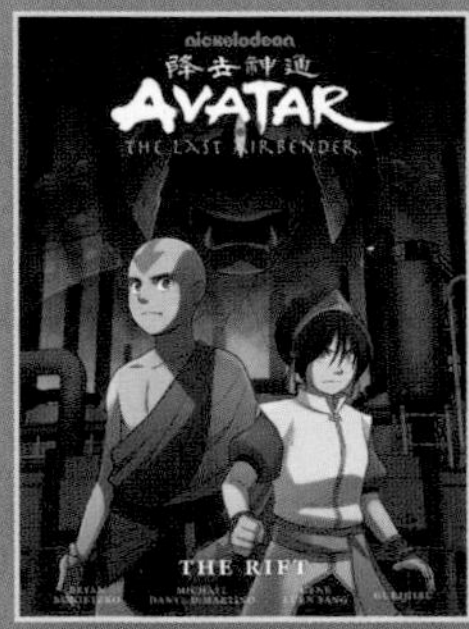

Avatar: The Last Airbender—The Rift Library Edition
978-1-61655-550-4 $39.99

Avatar: The Last Airbender—The Rift Part 1
978-1-61655-295-4 $12.99

Avatar: The Last Airbender—The Rift Part 2
978-1-61655-296-1 $12.99

Avatar: The Last Airbender—The Rift Part 3
978-1-61655-297-8 $12.99

Avatar: The Last Airbender—Smoke and Shadow Library Edition
978-1-50670-013-7 $39.99

Avatar: The Last Airbender—Smoke and Shadow Part 1
978-1-61655-761-4 $12.99

Avatar: The Last Airbender—Smoke and Shadow Part 2
978-1-61655-790-4 $12.99

Avatar: The Last Airbender—Smoke and Shadow Part 3
978-1-61655-838-3 $12.99

Avatar: The Last Airbender—North and South Library Edition
978-1-50670-195-0 $39.99

Avatar: The Last Airbender—North and South Part 1
978-1-50670-022-9 $12.99

Avatar: The Last Airbender—North and South Part 2
978-1-50670-129-5 $12.99

Avatar: The Last Airbender—North and South Part 3
978-1-50670-130-1 $12.99

Avatar: The Last Airbender—The Lost Adventures and Team Avatar Tales Library Edition
978-1-50672-274-0 $39.99

Avatar: The Last Airbender—The Lost Adventures
978-1-59582-748-7 $17.99

Avatar: The Last Airbender Chibis—Aang's Unfreezing Day
978-1-50672-661-8 $7.99

Avatar: The Last Airbender—Suki, Alone
978-1-50671-713-5 $12.99

Avatar: The Last Airbender—Toph Beifong's Metalbending Academy
978-1-50671-712-8 $12.99

Avatar: The Last Airbender—Katara and the Pirate's Silver
978-1-50671-711-1 $12.99

BE PART OF THE INCREDIBLE JOURNEY!

Check out the best-selling graphic novels and recapture the magic!

Avatar: The Last Airbender—The Art of the Animated Series
978-1-59582-504-9 $39.99

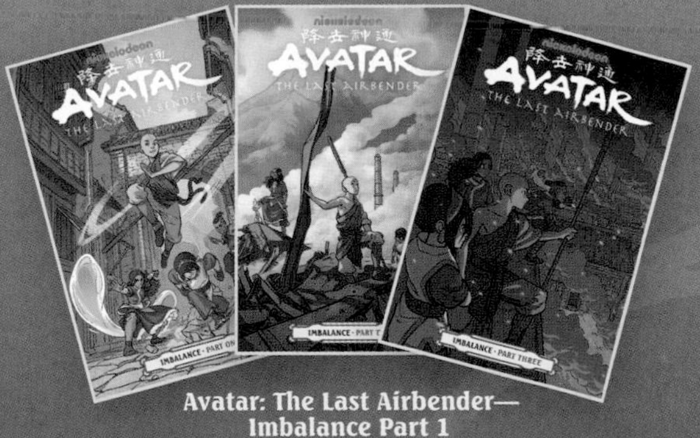

Avatar: The Last Airbender—Imbalance Part 1
978-1-50670-489-0 $12.99

Avatar: The Last Airbender—Imbalance Part 2
978-1-50670-652-8 $12.99

Avatar: The Last Airbender—Imbalance Part 3
978-1-50670-813-3 $12.99

Avatar: The Last Airbender—Imbalance Library Edition
978-1-50670-812-6 $39.99

AVAILABLE AT YOUR LOCAL COMICS SHOP OR BOOKSTORE! To find a comics shop in your area, visit comicshoplocator.com. For more information or to order direct, visit DarkHorse.com

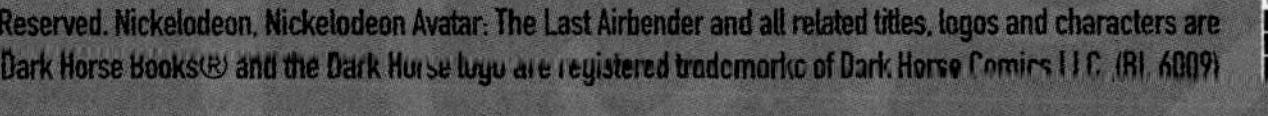